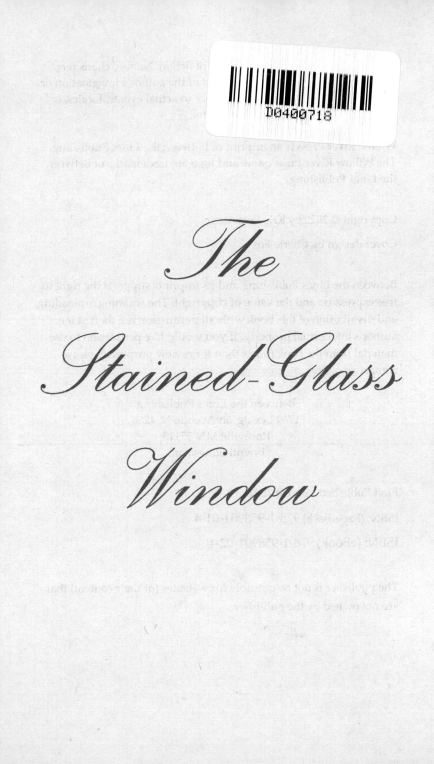

The

Stained-Glass

Window

Willow River Press is an imprint of Between the Lines Publishing. The Willow River Press name and logo are trademarks of Between the Lines Publishing.

Between the Lines Publishing
1769 Lexington Avenue N, #286
Roseville MN 55113
btwnthelines.com

First Published: August 2022

ISBN: (Paperback) 978-1-958901-01-4

ISBN: (eBook) 978-1-958901-02-1

The Stained-Glass Window

Kris Francoeur

Other titles by Kris Francoeur available from
Willow River Press

Tomorrow and Yesterday

Letting Go for Love

That Missed Call

For Paul, Ben, Ryan, Amie, Kayla, Linnea, Shane, Rowan, Shay, and Sora—thanks for always celebrating with me.

As always, for Sam, who believed.

Chapter 1

I stood in my brightly lit kitchen, stirring pasta into the boiling water. I was starved – ready to eat anything.

Yup, this was my life. Forgetting to eat until I was so hungry, I could eat anything. Forget about decent food; had there been chips in the house, I would have choked down a whole damn bag while the water boiled.

Why not eat like a normal person? Well, truth be told, I'm not exactly normal.

Three minutes were left on the timer, and everything else was ready. I had some chopped chicken with spinach, onions, and zucchini ready to be tossed with the pasta and some olive oil. A shower of Parmesan over the whole thing, and it would be a great dinner.

Dinner? Had I eaten lunch? Shit, I bet I didn't. My last meal had been an early morning cup of coffee and a banana. No wonder I was famished.

1

Taking a sip of wine, I tapped my foot as I contemplated eating crunchy pasta.

Just then, the phone rang. No, I thought, not now. I wanted food. My phone was on the table, so I couldn't see the caller ID. Whoever it was, they could wait. If it were important, they would leave a message or call back, buying me enough time to drain my pasta, toss my meal together, and sit down at the table. I could return the call once I got a few bites into me. Finally, Alexa sounded the timer. Once I dumped the pasta into the pan with everything else, I gave it a rudimentary stir and scooped most of it into a pasta bowl.

The blasted phone was ringing again. Still nope. I was grating the cheese over my bowl, ready to take it and my glass of wine to the table. Only then would I see who wanted to talk to me so badly.

At the table, I quickly ground a decent amount of black pepper onto my meal, then a dash of salt. I topped off my wine and took my first glorious bite. It may not have been fancy, and maybe not even that good, but it was ambrosia to me. No, not the gross marshmallow "salad," but the food of the Greek gods. In fact, it might have been the best meal I had ever eaten, or at least the best since yesterday, when I'd forgotten to eat then too.

Three bites later, I was ready to look at my phone. Two calls in quick succession, and as I looked at the screen, I realized they were both from James Lions. Hmm…Was he going to make my day or ruin it?

Just then, my phone lit up with a text. *Lil – call me!* It was James again. I took a sip, then hit call. He answered on the third ring. "About time," he said.

I smiled. James always made me smile. "I was making dinner. You could wait until I'd had a couple of bites."

"You should treat me better, you know that, right?"

That made me laugh. "I know. You're a prince to put up with me."

"Good to hear you say it."

"Always glad to make you happy." I took another bite, chewed, and swallowed. "So, what's up?"

"She's dead."

Those two words caught me off guard. I didn't know what to say. "When?" I croaked.

"Best guess? About two hours ago."

I took a sip of wine. "What happened?"

James, as always, acting like the lawyer he was, kept to the facts when talking with me about my Great-Aunt Helen, the evilest woman I knew. "She told Willy she was taking a nap before dinner. Willy helped her to bed. She laid down on top of the bedspread and told Willy to wake her when dinner was ready."

I interrupted. "Her normal four-thirty dinner, unless she had company to impress."

"Of course. When Willy got to her room, she knocked and knocked, and when there was no response, Willy opened the door and found her. The ME thinks it was a heart attack in her sleep – says it was instantaneous and painless."

I tried to maintain basic human decency. "I should be grateful for that."

James chuckled. "Lily, you don't need to put up a sweet front for my benefit. We both knew her well, so let's just say it's over."

I leaned back in my chair. "Amen." I pulled a notepad toward me. "So, what do I need to do?"

"For now? Nothing. Her wishes included no service, no event of any kind. Two weeks from now, we will have the formal reading of the will, and you need to attend that, but I can schedule it to fit what's best for you since it does have to be in New York. You already know what's in the will. God knows, she beat you over the head with it for decades."

That was an understatement. That old bitch had made her will a weapon of unparalleled power and cruelty. "And Willy? Please tell me she did something for Willy."

4

James sighed. "Not what anyone else would have done, that's for sure. Her health and dental insurance will be paid for the rest of her life, and she gets one year's salary, but after all she did, it certainly doesn't seem fair."

I took a bite, chewing slowly while I thought. "Okay," I said, "I can be in New York on the seventeenth."

"I'll make that work. Any specific time?"

"No, I'll drive up the night before. Could you book me at the Four Seasons?"

"You don't want to stay at the house?"

I laughed, but the sound was cold and devoid of joy, even to my own ears. "I'd just as soon throw a match on the place. I don't ever want to walk through that door again."

"I'll book you a suite there, the estate will pay for it."

"Thanks, James."

"And we'll have dinner that night?"

"Absolutely," I said. "How about room service and an enormous bottle of tequila?"

"Sounds like a plan."

After hanging up, I ate the rest of my dinner. James had been part of my life since I was sixteen. He was just ten years my senior and a good friend and confidante.

How the hell had he ever worked for her? No matter how much lawyers prided themselves on representing all walks of life, she was a lot to tolerate. But he had always managed to do it with professionalism, decency, and a sense of humor. Without him, I would have been terrified and isolated. When we got together, we dealt with business, then ate a great meal, drank too much, and had a platonic sleepover.

Shit. She was dead. I had waited for this day for as long as I could remember. Now she was finally gone, and I was not sure how I should feel.

Chapter 2

Two weeks later, I sat in James' office, already knowing most of what I was about to hear. After all, it had been brought up and used against me on a regular basis after my mom died.

I had dressed for the occasion. (I would like to say I am mature, not prone to sarcasm or wise-ass gestures, but that would be a lie; I have crafted sarcasm and wise-ass-ness into an art form. And yes, wise-ass-ness is a word. I am a highly successful writer, so I know words.)

Back to my outfit. On this auspicious occasion, I chose a severe black wool blazer with matching pencil pants and black stilettos. She hated stilettos. She called them "slut shoes." And then there was my blouse. Bright red silk with a neckline low enough to show some cleavage. After a quick hello hug, James gave me the once-over, his handsome face creased with a smile. It was obvious he was trying to contain his laughter. He shook his head. "Lil, you know she's dead, right? She can't see your red blouse."

I laughed. "It's the principle of the thing, James. You're supposed to wear black, or so she preached, when someone dies. And yet, to loosely quote *Moonstruck*, I always wanted to tell her she would die someday, and I would wear red to her funeral. Without a funeral, this is the best I could do."

"I understand the feeling," he chuckled.

"Why did you put up with her for all these years?" I said because I had always wanted to ask.

He motioned to a chair facing his desk. "Have a seat and I'll answer that."

I sat. He sat in his desk chair. I looked at his familiar tanned face and the blond hair I suspected he now lightened as he grew older. He was impeccably dressed by a matter of routine and always carried himself with a calm professionalism. He was a good friend—a damn good friend. Outside of his career, I knew he loved to hike and kayak, played a mean game of squash, and had been married to three gorgeous bimbos (most would call them socialites). He never stayed married long, always getting divorced and moving on to an even more beautiful, and younger, woman.

He tented his fingers. "She was a bitch, but as far as clients go, she wasn't that high maintenance. Her biggest tantrums were thrown over how to deny you your trust fund. She paid her bills, didn't waste my time with nonsense, and was cold but not crazy." He smiled sardonically. "To put it simply, she paid for my house in Aspen, and at least one of my divorces."

"Okay, that makes sense." I leaned back and took a deep breath. "Let's get this over with."

He nodded. "Want coffee? Water? Whiskey?"

I smiled. "Black coffee now. Tequila tonight."

He buzzed for his assistant, who presented our coffee in two gorgeous bone china teacups on delicate matching saucers. Perfect sugar cookies were neatly displayed on a small plate in the center of the tray. The presentation of the coffee tray was spectacular. Just because I chose not to live like the dead bitch didn't mean I couldn't appreciate some of the finer things. "Thank you," I said.

After he took a sip, James opened the folder in front of him. "Let's do this."

I sat and listened while he read me Great-Aunt Helen's will. The content was much as I had expected it, with a few predictably nasty digs in the commentary she left to be read with it. As I listened, it was clear that no matter how much she would have preferred I get nothing, she hated charities more, so in the end, she chose to leave most of it to me. The brownstone in Manhattan. The cottage on Cape Cod. The furnishings in both. Her season tickets to the New York Yankees (one of the only fun things she ever took part in regularly).

Then there were Helen's financial holdings. I listened as James rattled them off, not really caring. I was already more than comfortably well off, so this was nice but not life changing. I would rather have not inherited a thing and still had my mom.

Wait. I should probably explain myself. Yes, you could say I'm wealthy. That came to be out of three distinct factors. First, my grandfather Alfred, whom I never met, had only one child – my mom. When he died, he left Mom everything, but she had just recently died – a fact her own father was not even aware of when he passed. She had no contact with her parents once she found out she was pregnant with me. All told, Alfred's estate passed to me by way of a trust I inherited in full at the age of twenty-five.

Then… well, not to toot my own horn, but I am a successful writer. Three *New York Times* Best Sellers for fiction in the last three years. I have another coming out soon, and I don't mind saying the advance on it was six-figures.

I'm also well off because my ex-husband and I both did well and invested well. We split everything fifty-fifty when we divorced. At that point, he made more than I did, but everything was still split down the middle. I did not need a damn thing from Helen, that was for sure.

I suddenly realized James was looking at me in amusement, clearly waiting for an answer on something. "What," I said, "did I zone out?"

"Yes," he said patiently. "Welcome back."

I ignored the second comment. People have been making comments about my daydreaming since I was a toddler. "What did I miss?"

"That you also inherited a house in Vermont."

Okay, now that shocked me. "What the hell are you talking about? She didn't have a house in Vermont."

He shrugged. "I don't know if she ever went there, but she *did* own a house, and always had, at least as long as I knew her."

Vermont? Holy shit... I had lived there from the age of three until I was thirteen when my mom died. I had never gone back, although I had only good memories of it. I had been happy and felt loved there. Wow, Vermont. "Where? What kind of house?"

"I don't really know. I only know it's up in the northeastern part of the state, and no one has lived there in years. It's got fifty acres and there's a pond big enough for a dock."

I tried to recall Vermont's geography. "In the Northeast Kingdom?"

He shrugged. "How the hell would I know? But it is on Kingdom Road, so maybe."

"And why did she have this house?"

He rolled his eyes, clearly amused that I would ask such a question. "Why did she have anything she had? Because she wanted to, and she could. As for this particular property, I have no clue beyond that."

I rubbed my forehead, thinking about what I had expected to hear since the day James called to say she was gone. This was not anything I saw coming. I took a deep breath. "I'll keep the house on the Cape. As far as the house here, I want to let Willy live there as long as she wants, with the agreement the estate will pay utilities, taxes, and upkeep. If she has other plans, I want to sell it. And as far as its contents, the only things I want are the grandfather clock and the piano in the parlor. The rest can be sold with the house." Now I was on a roll. "And Willy is to be paid her full salary for the rest of her life."

James was taking notes as I spoke, so I continued. "The Yankees tickets can be passed on to David. He loves the Yankees, and that old bitch always knew I was a Sox fan."

James rolled his eyes. "You're giving season tickets to your ex-husband?"

"Yes."

"I never have understood your relationship." He grinned, "I would never give my exes something that valuable without the court mandating it."

"We have a unique relationship, you know that."

"True." He paused. "What about the Vermont house?"

"Fuck." I sighed. "I'll take a drive up there to check it out next weekend. I expect I'll be calling you to put it on the market, but I'll at least go see it first."

He nodded. "Do you want us to find you a place to stay up there?"

"Yes, please. Just, for God's sake, no bed and breakfast, or anything where small talk is expected."

He tried to keep from laughing. "Of course."

Chapter 3

The next morning, I stood at the door of my hotel room, wrapped in one of their fluffy, overpriced robes. James was ready to leave, dressed to the nines and ready to go about his professional day. He leaned down and pulled me into his arms for a tight squeeze. "Love you, Lil."

"Likewise." I leaned against him briefly. James was one of my few close friends, and I always felt a bit melancholy when our times together came to a close. "Thanks for everything."

"My pleasure." He kissed the top of my head. "Text me when you leave and when you get there."

"Yes, mother."

"Just do it."

I reached up to straighten his tie. "I will. And thanks for taking care of all the other stuff."

14

"No worries. Willy was ecstatic when I told her you were going to stop by to see her today. Thanks for doing that."

"I've always loved Willy, that was never an issue."

"I know. But I also know how hard you've worked to avoid going to the house. Thanks for doing it one more time."

Four hours later, I was on the interstate, headed back to Boston. Seeing Willy had been a treat, as was her reaction when she learned there was no need to move or find another job. After being at Helen's beck and call for more than thirty years, it was the least I could do for her. The elderly black woman had been my only friend and confidante on the few occasions I had to stay with Helen. Her kindness, her sense of humor, and her cookies had made my life bearable in those days. I wanted her to be well cared for every second of the remainder of her life.

The drive was uneventful, and by the time I pulled into my parking space, I was bored and lonely.

I slogged up the stairs to the front door. First, I'd throw a load of laundry in, and then I'd order an early dinner of takeout.

Standing at the kitchen counter with the menus, I picked up the phone and hit speed dial. The voice was warm. "Hey, how was New York?"

"Well, it was good for you. You are now a proud season ticket holder for the Yankees."

"Holy shit! Really, Lil?"

"Yeah."

"Thank you, sweetie."

"You're welcome." I bit my lower lip. "Hey, can I come over?"

His voice deepened. "Megan is away."

"I know."

"Ah, *that* kind of visit."

I leaned my head against the cabinet. Damn it. I wish I had more willpower. "Yes."

"Come on over."

Chapter 4

It took only five minutes of brisk walking to reach what used to be my front door. I still had a key, so I rang the bell and let myself in, knowing David would still be in his top-floor office of the brownstone.

"Do you want something?" I called up the stairs.

"Grab a bottle of wine, will you?"

"Sure." Red wine. David thought white wine was a sin. I walked into the kitchen, grabbed two glasses and a bottle of Merlot, knowing there was a corkscrew up in his office.

I climbed the stairs. As I expected, he was at his desk under the dormer, his dark hair slightly longer than he preferred, which always happened when he was going through final edits. He got so involved he forgot to get it cut. I smiled. Who was I to comment on his hair? I kept mine long, so I didn't have to worry about going to the salon when I was busy. "Hey," I said.

He turned to look at me. His eyes were warm. "Hey, baby."

I walked toward him, carefully putting the glasses on his desk before I leaned down to kiss him.

As my lips touched his, one of his hands reached up to cup my head, pulling me closer, while the other slid under my t-shirt, caressing the bare skin of my ribcage. "Welcome back," he growled.

Don't judge me. It's not what it seems. Well, yes, it is. And it isn't. It's really complicated and painfully simple.

I met David on the first day of our freshman year of college. He was the hottest guy I had ever seen, and he seemed smitten with me too. We were lovers by Christmas.

Six months later, we were engaged. We got married the day after we graduated and moved to Boston to start our writing careers. We were writing partners, business partners, and we edited for each other. We had a great marriage and loved each other deeply.

So, what was the problem? Well… David didn't want just me in his bed; he wanted an open marriage. Then, he wanted to take my best friend Megan as his lover while still with me. (She wanted that too.)

I was the holdout. Although I had come from the least traditional of family backgrounds, I was really into the idea of a traditional marriage. I could not handle the fact that he wanted other lovers. We went into counseling. And he still wanted an open marriage. We tried; it didn't work. Finally, we divorced. It was more than amicable. We split everything down the middle, stayed writing and business partners, and about six months after our divorce and his marriage to Megan, we became lovers again. Now, David has two women outside of his marriage – me and someone named Rosa, who lives in Manhattan. Megan has three other lovers – in Boston, New York, and Rome.

The weird thing? It works for them. They have even been known to go on vacation with their other lovers. They all know each other, so there seems to be no jealousy, and no one is getting hurt.

At first, the idea of being with David again while he was married to someone else seemed wrong. Then it didn't. Now it seems natural and normal. We love each other, the sex is phenomenal, and yet comforting, and there is no need to pretend about anything.

Two hours after that first kiss, I was sitting on the couch in his office, completely naked. I felt more relaxed than I had been in days and was eating Chinese food from the boxes while I sipped wine with my equally naked ex-husband.

David looked at me. "Vermont? Seriously?"

"Yeah, an old house on fifty acres with a pond; no one has lived there in years. I'm going to drive up there to see it before I decide what to do with it."

"Have you looked it up on Google Earth?"

"No." Duh, why didn't I think of that?

He reached over and grabbed his laptop. "What's the address?"

In less than a minute, we were looking at a street view image of my new property. "Looks like a stiff wind would knock it over," I remarked.

He nodded. "It does, but it also has great lines." He pointed. "Look at that sun porch. What a great writing space that could be."

"You trying to get me to move?"

"Hell no," he laughed, "I hope you fix it up, so we have a great space to work when we are marathoning edits."

"Always thinking, you are."

He gathered up the now-empty boxes. "I am. And now I'm thinking we should work off some of the calories we just consumed."

And we did.

Chapter 5

Three days later, I sat outside of a Dunkin' Donuts and sighed. What the hell was I thinking, driving up to Vermont to look at some old dump Helen left me? She had probably done it out of spite. She was luring me up here so I could be attacked by a bear and left for dead.

I got out of the car and walked into the store. A big cup of coffee would clear my mind, and a chocolate donut would make me a nicer person, for a while, at least.

Forty-five minutes later, I pulled into the driveway of my weekend Airbnb. The cottage was adorable – one story, covered in weathered wooden shingles, beautiful trim, and glorious gardens full of early spring blooms.

The key was exactly where the owner said it would be. I carried my bag inside, smiling as my eyes landed on

21

the small wood stove and a bouquet of wildflowers with a bottle of wine next to it. How sweet!

I quickly unpacked and ate a yogurt I had brought for the road before grabbing my keys and heading out to see the mystery house.

It only took ten minutes to reach the property, and it was a beautiful drive. I had forgotten how spectacular Vermont was, and no matter what I decided to do with the house, I vowed to get up here more often.

The dirt driveway was steep and unmarked. Slowly, I turned up it, hoping my car was up to the task. (I remembered my mom saying anyone in Vermont should have four-wheel drive, and my car did not fit this category.) The path seemed to wind around the back of the hill, and then I was there.

The house was old. Possibly ancient. It sat on the top of the hill, overlooking the valley below. Was it Victorian? No, not really. Well, sort of, maybe. It had a round tower on one side, and the other had a huge all-season porch encased in glass – the sun porch that had caught David's eye. There was a deep, covered front porch that seemed perfect for looking out at the world when one did not want to be totally inside.

Someone must have been hired to keep the grounds up, at least to a certain extent. While the lawn needed mowing, and what had been the flower gardens were an overgrown mess now, you could see that the property hadn't been ignored completely over the years.

Beside the house was an impressively sizable barn with a slate roof. The red slate stood out from the traditional dark gray slabs, and they had been arranged to display the date of establishing the homestead, reading a clear 1842.

I walked slowly around the house and came to the pond. The pond sat below the house, and in the sunlight, the clear water sparkled. It was a beautiful little pond. From the porch or the hill, you could see for miles. The distant mountains were strikingly beautiful. Wow.

That was it. I knew at that moment that I wanted this place. I wanted to bring it back to its former glory and live in it. I was going to have a house with a view. I had no idea why it had been given to me, but it had, and I suddenly felt filled with an unexpected sense of hope and happiness. I was going to have a *home* again.

The key to the front door was in my pocket. James had sent a building inspector to be sure it was structurally sound prior to my arrival. Cautiously, I unlocked the front door and entered the foyer, gazing at the curved staircase that climbed to the second floor.

How could Helen have owned this gem and not done anything with it?

I walked from room to room, each one better than the last.

Finally, I came to a large set of double doors. Opening them, I found what must have been the master bedroom. Well, now it was going to be mine. A wall of windows looked out over the front porch and had a view of the mountains that took my breath away.

I was in love. This house was *me*, through and through. This was where I was going to live and work for the rest of my life.

Now I needed to figure out how to fix it up.

Chapter 6

A week later, I drove the interstate again, this time in my new Subaru, pulling a small trailer behind me. James' voice came through the speakers. "I still don't understand why you don't hire someone to do the work, and you could stay in Boston until the place is habitable."

"No. I told you, I want to be there to oversee the process. I'm meeting with a contractor tomorrow, the one you found for me. If he works out, my plan is to have him work on the kitchen and the first-floor bathroom, followed by my office space and my bedroom. Once the office is ready, I'll sleep on the pullout couch. Then I'll have him go through the place room by room."

"It's going to cost a fortune."

"Probably, but as you know, I have the money."

Back at the same Airbnb, I unpacked what I would need for the near future. I wanted to move into the house as soon as I could, but at least I was nearby while renovations took place.

The next morning, I was sitting on the front porch of the house, admiring the view, when a big pickup truck came up the driveway. My potential contractor was not what I expected. He was well over six feet tall and built like a Greek god. His hair was black as coal, and his eyes were bright blue; I admit I swallowed hard when I saw him. He was fucking gorgeous. I don't know why, but I was expecting an older man with a beer belly and a tool belt. This guy looked like he could be yachting off the Cape. Wow.

I gave my head a quick shake. I needed to get my mind straight to negotiate. After all, this was a huge project.

He extended his hand. "Ms. Brannan?"

"Please, call me Lily."

"Lily it is. I'm Tom, Tom Givens."

"Nice to meet you."

He looked around. "Wow, I've heard about this place, but I've never been up here. The view is everything people said it was."

We walked and talked, and Tom took copious notes. Finally, we sat down on the porch. He flipped through his pad. "Look, to be honest, doing this project in sections will make it more expensive in the long run; it would require me to jump around a bit, and that always takes more time, therefore more money."

"I know, but I want to move in as soon as I can, so it's the only way I see feasible."

Tom shrugged. "As long as you understand, it's fine with me."

I looked at him intently. "I'd also prefer your best estimate, and then updates every two weeks on how close you think things are running."

"I can do that." He stood. "Let me get to work on that and I'll get back to you by this time tomorrow."

"Thanks, that's great."

Tom drove away, and I sat for a while longer. There were so many things I needed to put into place. Next on my list was to get internet service so I could work. It was time to get moving.

By late afternoon, I had secured a communications package, complete with a landline, internet, and cable; I had sent a well water sample off for testing and made an appointment with a chimney sweep. I was tired and hungry and remembered seeing a pizzeria in town. I was going to get a pizza and sit and write for a while.

While I waited for my pie to be made, I scrolled through emails, sending a few responses. I was so intent on what I was doing I didn't realize a man had been watching me from across the room. Finally, when I realized he was looking at me each time I looked up, I put my phone down and smiled. "Hello," I said.

He stood up and walked over to my table. This was the second man I had seen in one day, and he was just as beautiful as the first. Damn, they grew hotties up here.

The man gestured to the other side of my booth. "May I?"

"Sure."

He sat and held out one hand. "Roberto Romano."

"Lily Brannan."

"The author?"

I nodded, always pleased to be recognized. "Yes."

"And what are you doing in our small town?" He had a slight accent, Italian, it seemed.

"I have a house here and I'm having some renovations done."

"Oh, I see."

"And you? What do you do?"

He smiled, and for a moment, the word *dandy* crossed my mind. While Tom had the light eyes, Roberto had longish pitch-black hair and eyes almost as dark. His skin tone echoed the accent. My guess was he had been born elsewhere. "I teach at the college," he said.

"And what do you teach?"

"Italian."

"Impressive." Although I spoke Spanish and French, Italian had always eluded me. Suddenly it hit me, duh, it was his native language, so it wasn't as impressive as I'd thought. I kept that last thought to myself.

"Thank you."

We chatted for a few more minutes until my order was called. "That's me," I said, "I need to go." I smiled. "It was nice to meet you, Roberto."

"You too, Lily." He paused. "Forgive me for being so bold, but would you like to join me for a drink tomorrow night? To welcome you to the area, of course."

Wow, when was the last time a stranger asked me out? A *long* time ago. Of course, that might be in part due to the fact that I basically barely leave my house because I write around the clock. Anyway, his question felt good. "I'd like that," I said.

"Great. I'll meet you at Zebra's tomorrow at six?"

"Sounds good, I'll be there."

The next evening, I dressed with more care than usual. I'm confident in my appearance; after all, I've spent a lot of time on things like headshots for my books, and I know I'm attractive. I have a better-than-average body, and my eyes and hair are admittedly fabulous. (Just like my mom's.)

I pulled on a pair of black capris and topped them with a soft blue blouse that accentuated my eyes. A little bit of makeup, and I was ready. Late spring in Vermont could be warm and then cold, all in the space of about ten minutes if my memory served me correctly, so I also grabbed a sweater to take with me.

I walked into Zebra's nervously. My social life sucks, so doing something like this felt foreign.

Roberto was waiting for me just inside the door. He smiled and leaned down to kiss my cheek. "Lily, it's so good to see you. You look beautiful."

I wanted to tell him he was beautiful too, but that seemed too much for a first drink. "It's a pleasure to see you too."

One drink turned into two. Drinks turned into dinner and then a walk through the quiet streets while Roberto told me stories about the town's history and its residents. By the time we left the restaurant, we were holding hands.

What the hell was wrong with me? I never jumped into anything, yet here I was, out with a man I had just met the day before, and now I was wondering how quickly I could get him into my bed. God, he was so gorgeous. And sexy. And sweet and attentive. His little European mannerisms made him even hotter, like when he picked up my hand and kissed the back of it during dinner.

Finally, we were back at Zebra's parking lot. I leaned against my car. "Thank you, I had a great time."

"Me too, Lily. Would it be too much if I asked you to do it again tomorrow night? I have a late class but could meet you around eight for a late dinner."

"Why don't you come to my place, and I'll make us dinner?"

He smiled and reached out to stroke my cheek. I thought I might pass out right then and there. He was doing things to my insides that should be illegal or at least controlled.

"*Bellissima*, I would love that, but I'm afraid it's too soon." Before I could feel like a complete ass, he leaned closer, his lips nearly brushing mine. "I would love to come to your house, but there, I know I won't be able to control how much I want you, and you are far too precious for a fling. I want us to take our time."

What the hell do I say to that, I thought. "Oh," was the only response I could come up with.

"What, *bella*? What is the matter?" He pulled my hand to his lips as he spoke, kissing it lingeringly.

Jesus, what could I say? This amazing, gorgeous man was saying he liked me enough to *not* go to bed with me. Was this real? The men I know aren't that deep, or subtle, for that matter. I wasn't really sure how to feel. "Nothing's the matter, Roberto."

"Berto," he corrected. "I thought you agreed to call me Berto, my *bella*."

"Berto. It's just unusual, that's all."

"You mean it's unusual that a man would believe you to be such a treasure that you should be treated like the princess you are? That's a problem?"

Well, shit. When he put it like that, it sounded so good. "No, of course it's not a problem."

"Good, then let me take you to dinner at Hemingway's, and then we can go for another walk."

"I'd love that."

By the time I got back to the cottage, I was tired. It had been a wonderful evening, romantic and fun. Wow, maybe coming back to Vermont was exactly what I had needed all along.

Stepping inside, I dropped my bag, changed into pajamas, and turned on my laptop, which I had not checked all day. There was an email from Tom with his estimate.

I read the estimate over and over. It was more than fair. Shit, having owned a brownstone in Boston and renovated it, I was incredibly pleased by the cost of labor up here. I could do this.

I emailed him back. *Hi, Tom, this looks great. When can you start, and what do you require for a deposit? Thanks so much, Lily.*

The next two weeks were a blur of excitement, emotion, and physical exertion as I settled into an exhausting routine. I was up each day long before sunrise, writing for hours. Then I headed over to the house and worked on cleaning inside or cleaning up around the property. I checked in with Tom and his crew, then worked until my body cried uncle. I headed back to the cottage for a few more hours of writing, got cleaned up, and then spent the evenings with Berto.

In the weeks since we met, we progressed beyond handholding, but not as far as I would have liked. He was clear on the fact that he found me attractive, and he treated me like a precious jewel, like his princess. Flowers arrived with a sweet note several times a week.

When our schedules didn't mesh, we had long talks on the phone and an occasional video chat.

I knew he liked me. I knew he found me attractive. But he would not come to my place or take me to his. Our dates were in public, or at least, not at our homes. We sat by the lake one afternoon with a picnic. We went to the movies. But when the evening was over, he kissed me tenderly and said good night.

I had tried to move past this phase a couple of times. And with that sweet gentility, he turned me down, saying it was still too soon. He whispered that it would be worth the wait, and I believed him, but damn, I was in an unprecedented state of sexual frustration.

I thought of taking a quick run to Boston a few times or seeing if David would drive up for the weekend, but that seemed wrong. I mean, I would be asking someone, him or me, to drive for hours just because I couldn't get my new boyfriend to take me to bed. No, visiting David was out of the question. I needed to take things into my own hands, so to speak, and hope that Berto would be overcome with lust.

A week passed, and there was a day when I decided to forego work at the house, as I needed to focus on some editing. I had just met my goal for the day and stood up to stretch when my cell rang. "Hey, Tom."

"Lily! How are you? It was weird without you here today."

I smiled. "Yeah, I bet the guys really missed having me underfoot."

That made him laugh. "They love your energy and your excitement about the house, and the beer you bring on Fridays makes them happy as hell."

"Well, good," I said.

"Hey, I wanted to tell you the kitchen and bathroom are done. We finished them today."

"Really?" I was thrilled. "I thought you said it would be sometime early next week."

"I had two extra sets of hands today, and we really bulled and jammed. Wanna come see it?"

I was already grabbing my keys. "I'm on my way."

Walking through the door to the kitchen took my breath away. It was exactly what I had always wanted. I mean, I don't cook all that often, but when I do, I'm pretty good. This was a space designed by me, for me, and it was gorgeous. With my height, I had designed the space, so I didn't spend all my time on my tiptoes trying to reach things. A huge center island held a cooktop, a sink, and a large area for people to sit on the high stools. The six-burner stove sat proudly against the back wall, with counters on either side for things to cool if needed.

Yes, maybe the cooktop and the big stove were a bit much, but when I cook, I like lots of space, and finally, in this kitchen, I would have it. My collection of cookbooks written by Julia Child would be put to good use here, and I couldn't wait! The entire room was painted in a soft, warm ivory color, with the cabinets being a dark blue. The countertops were a speckled gray. Once my dishes arrived, I would put everything exactly where I wanted it, and I couldn't wait.

I peeked into the bathroom and felt the same rush of joy all over again. The old, decrepit bathroom that held only a small sink, toilet, and a shower so small even I would have struggled to shower there were gone. Tom and his crew had worked miracles. They had knocked out a wall to an unused closet, and now the space was large, light, and airy. A pedestal sink was nestled in the corner, right by the windows looking out over what would eventually turn back into flower gardens. They had built a wall so that the now amply sized shower was hidden as you walked in, and floor to ceiling shelves would eventually be filled with fluffy towels to welcome anyone who wanted to use them. Here the colors were muted blues and yellows, and the room was welcoming and relaxing, just like I had envisioned.

I turned to him and could feel the smile on my face. "Tom, I don't know what to say. It is perfect. I can't believe you pulled this together in such a short time. Thank you."

He was the epitome of a hot guy who did hard physical labor, dressed in his faded jeans and a fitted navy-blue tee. He was fucking gorgeous, and he gave me a lazy grin. "I am so glad you like it. I'm pleased with how it came out."

"You should be."

He gestured to the fridge. "I put a bottle of champagne in there so you could celebrate."

I was touched. "Thank you." Suddenly, I felt shy. "Would you stay and have a glass with me?"

He looked uncomfortable, and I wondered if I had put my foot in my mouth. Did he have a wife or girlfriend at home? He wasn't wearing a ring, but did that really mean anything? He worked with his hands, so maybe he took it off when on the job. "How will your boyfriend feel about you having a drink with me?" he said.

"What?"

His eyes never left mine. "Everyone knows you're seeing Roberto Romano. I'm happy to have a drink with you, Lily, I'd love to. But I also don't want to cause a problem between the two of you."

I had to stifle a smile. Okay, this hunky sweetheart was worrying about stepping on Berto's toes, and my ex-husband had wanted to have an open marriage. I sure knew how to find interesting people on both ends of the spectrum. "He's not my boyfriend," I said. "We see each other but it's not like we're serious."

"Really?" He tipped his head as he gazed at me. "That's not what I thought."

"Really. We have drinks, sometimes dinner, but it is no more than that, at least right now. And besides, I'm a grown woman, I can have a drink with whomever I want to, period." I took a deep breath. "Please, stay."

He nodded. "Sure, that would be great. Let me step out to make a quick call, I'll be right back." He grinned. "I took the liberty of washing some glasses, just in case you had a friend join you."

"Thanks."

Tom was back in a few short minutes. When he reappeared, I opened the fridge and smiled as I found a plate of fruit and cheese beside the champagne. "Wow," I said.

He looked pleased with himself. "Well, it was my idea, but I admit I have a helper who puts things together for me."

I had to ask; I needed to know. "Wife? Girlfriend?"

He shook his head, and for a moment, I saw what seemed to be a flash of sadness in his eyes. "Mother," he said.

"Oh." What was I supposed to say to that? Was he a mama's boy?

He took over, quickly and efficiently opening the bottle and filling two flutes. "Lily," he said, "welcome home. It's not done yet but it's getting there."

I clinked my glass with his. "Thanks to you." I took a sip and then popped a strawberry into my mouth. "Your mom knows how to pick fruit. Please thank her for me."

"I will." He took a sip. "Go ahead and ask," he said.

By now, we were both sitting on stools at the kitchen island. I was facing him, and his eyes glowed warmly in the soft light of the overhead lantern. Shit, he was gorgeous, and he didn't seem to have a woman, other than his mother, in his life. "What do you mean? Ask what?" I said.

He chuckled. "Admit it. You're wondering if I'm a mama's boy, right?"

That made me laugh, and I was momentarily afraid champagne would shoot out of my nose. "Okay, so maybe I was. So, well, are you?"

He shook his head. "No, my mom raised two independent sons and one even more independent

39

daughter, mostly on her own. Our dad died when I was four."

"I'm sorry. My mom died when I was thirteen and I never knew my dad."

"Then I'm sorry too."

"Sorry, I interrupted. Please continue."

"When I started this business, my plan was to get into the big commercial construction and make a fortune. But then my brother and his wife were killed, leaving my nephew without parents at only two months old."

"Shit!"

"Yeah. My sister lives out in California, and is, literally, a stunt double. She's constantly on the road and works crazy hours. My mom was going through breast cancer when Jimmy was killed, and there was no one on the maternal side. So, I adopted my nephew, and I bought the house next door to my mother. She helps with my son and with things like bringing champagne when the job is done, or in your case, the first section is done."

Wow. Taking in a baby and adopting him as a single guy. That was ballsy. "And your son?"

His eyes lit up, and I could immediately see how much he loved his son. "He's four now. He's a little hellion—smart as can be, independent, loves to help. He's a great little guy."

"He's lucky to have you."

40

"Nah, I'm the lucky one. Before him, I was too focused on making it big, and I was doing it. But I also was selling my soul to work on projects I hated. He made me recall there's more to life; that there's nothing better than playing trucks in the dirt with him."

I tipped my head, now seeing Tom in a new light. "I'd like to meet him," I said. The strange thing? As soon as the words came out of my mouth, I realized how very much truth was behind them.

"I'd like that too." He grinned. "When we get to the outside work, he comes to help sometimes. Sometimes he creates more work than we expect, but he loves to be part of the crew."

"Cool." I shrugged. "And he can't be worse at gardening than I am, so we can help each other."

We polished off the bottle of champagne and ate the fruit and cheese platter while we talked and laughed. Finally, Tom stood up. "Okay, I need to head home."

I stood and wobbled slightly. It made him smile. "Did you eat anything today other than what you just had?"

I shook my head. "No, I was working and forgot to eat. I do that sometimes."

That made him chuckle. "Jesus," he said, "you've got to be all of a hundred pounds soaking wet, and you just had half a bottle of champagne on an empty stomach."

"I'm one-oh-nine," I corrected.

"What?" He sounded confused.

"One hundred and nine," I said. "That's what I weigh."

He held out his hand. "Thanks for the clarification. Now come on, I'll give you a ride back to the cottage, and will get you tomorrow to pick up your car."

I was shocked. "I can drive myself."

"No, city girl, you can't. You're buzzed, and driving on these roads, when you still don't know them that well, isn't a good idea. Come on."

He was right. "Fine," I muttered.

As Tom drove me to my cottage, he told me about the places we were passing. As opposed to when Berto had walked me through town, Tom's information was funny, personal, and told me a lot more about the community I was joining.

He pulled up to the cottage and parked. "Okay," he said, "here you go. Now get some more food and some sleep."

I smiled, feeling strangely protected. "I will, thanks."

"I will be up at the house for a bit tomorrow morning. Do you want me to get you on my way, so you can get your car? Otherwise, I can take you back later in the day."

"On your way would be great. Just text me when you are headed this way."

"Will do."

"Night, Tom. Thanks."

"My pleasure."

Walking inside, I felt almost giddy. That had been fun. Silly fun. We had talked about all sorts of things and laughed. And those laughs were needed, that was for sure.

Just then, my phone rang. "Berto!"

His tone was curt, something I had never experienced before. "Where have you been?" he said.

"What do you mean?"

"I have been calling you for hours. Where have you been?"

(Okay, now let me be clear. My mother used to say, "I'm single and over 21—No one gets to ask me where I've been." And frankly, that's been my motto too.)

I took a deep breath, so I didn't snap at him. "Berto, they finished the kitchen and bathroom at the house today, so I went to see it."

"And that took hours? What, did you need to spend time with that contractor?"

Ew. The way he said *contractor* made it sound like a near-obscenity. Ouch. "Berto, I don't like your tone — your tone toward me, and your tone about Tom."

"And I don't like my woman being off with another man."

Now my temper was coming to the surface. It takes me a while to get mad, but when it happens, well, let's just say that when I was a teenager, my temper usually involved physical altercations. "I'm not your woman," I said. "We are seeing each other, but that does not mean I'm your possession. I can be with whomever I want." I took a deep breath. "Good night, Berto."

I hung up and turned my phone off.

An hour later, as I undressed and changed into a t-shirt and soft shorts to sleep, I thought about my evening. I'd had such a great time with Tom, and yet, now, it was tarnished because of Berto being such an ass.

I looked at my reflection in the bathroom mirror. "Men! Jesus, why do they have to be so confusing?"

My mirror image didn't reply. With a huff, I stomped off to bed.

Chapter 7

The next day, when I returned to the house, sitting in the front seat of Tom's truck, there was an enormous bouquet of roses waiting for me on the front steps with a note.

Bella mia, I am so sorry for how I acted. The idea of you being away from me for even a minute makes me crazy, and to think you were spending time with another man was more than I could handle. Please forgive me – your Berto.

Tom raised an eyebrow as he looked at the display. "What did he do that he feels he needs to apologize with flowers?"

That made me laugh. "He was an ass last night about why he couldn't reach me." Before Tom could say anything, I held up one hand. "Don't say it. I know you were worried that us hanging out last night would be a

45

problem for him, but he doesn't own me, as I reminded him last night."

"Why don't you go call him?"

"Nope." By then, I had decided to let him sit and spin for a while. "He can be patient for a while."

"Suit yourself."

I stalked off to my office and put my phone away to make Berto wait to hear from me. A bouquet of flowers was not enough for how he'd acted, right?

Okay, I let him wait for like an hour. Then I called him, let him grovel, and accepted his invitation for dinner at a small Mexican place in the next town over.

That night, I dressed with less care than normal, needing to show him that while I was interested, I wasn't putting in a lot of effort because I was still mad.

As I got out of my car, Berto came right over, holding out his hands to me. When I slipped mine into his, he lifted them, kissing each of my palms in turn. With that, I melted. Yes, he'd been an ass, but that was so sweet and sexy; how could I possibly stay mad?

"Berto."

"My Lily, I have waited all day to see you." He dipped his head in embarrassment. "I am so sorry for how I acted, my darling. Please forgive me."

"Forgiven and forgotten." I stretched up to kiss his cheek. "Thank you for the flowers, they are beautiful."

"Not half as beautiful as you, my princess."

After that, Berto had been incredibly careful not to upset me, but he also had been more demonstrative. It was nice, but still, if he cared so much, why wasn't he trying to take it to the next level?

Tom's crew had finished my office on the sun porch, the dining room, and parlor. The sun porch was spectacular and functional. They'd refinished the built-in shelves on the inner wall and repaired the damage to the windows that filled two complete walls. Now my desk would sit in the front corner, nestled between the windows and the bookshelves. I'd have a view and a place for all of my writing stuff. I could feel the space inspiring me, and all I wanted to do was write there. Each day, the house had more life injected into it. Today, I was officially moving in and setting myself up in the new office. Now, I could sleep on the pullout for a while if it meant being in my own house, so I had moved out of the rented cottage first thing this morning.

No, it wasn't just a house. It was my own *home*. This was my home now, and I couldn't wait to fully settle in.

The next morning, I was up long before sunrise, making a batch of blueberry muffins and brewing extra coffee for the guys. Over the last weeks, I had gotten to know the crew and really liked them. They made me laugh, and they were impressed I was a writer. (But not too impressed, since I couldn't do a lot of practical things.) They didn't worry about offending me. It was fun.

After joining the guys for muffins and coffee, I settled into my office; my writing table was already set up exactly where I wanted it. I would set up the rest of the office later in the day, but overnight I had figured out a plot issue in my latest work. I couldn't wait to get to my writing.

Five pages in, I was cruising. When the writing comes easy, I can't work fast enough or long enough. Time melts away, and it was happening in a big way.

Five more pages, and I was elated. This was fabulous. I stretched my shoulders, knowing I should stand for a bit. Reaching down, I hit the button to raise the desk, so I could stand and work. Just then, I heard Tom's voice. "Lily," he called.

"In my office." I loved saying that. This was the most perfect writing space I could ever imagine for myself.

His voice sounded off. "You should come see this."

Okay, I guess I needed to go see him. "Where are you?"

"In the front bedroom."

I hurried up the stairs. Whatever it was, I wanted to see it quickly and get back to work. "What is it?"

His voice still sounded weird to me. "Come in here, please."

God, I prayed it wasn't something gross that he wanted to show me. I mean, I have a fairly strong stomach for gore, but I would scream like a little girl if it were something like a bunch of dead rats in the wall.

I walked into what would be my bedroom with an odd sense of foreboding. There was now a gaping hole in the wallboard, which I had known was going to happen as they rewired the room. But under that wallboard was a piece of what looked to be stained glass.

"What the hell is that?" I said, my voice cracking with visceral shock.

"A window. But there wasn't a window here. It's like it was just hidden between the interior and exterior walls." Tom carefully extracted the large piece and took two steps so the sun's rays could stream through the panes.

The last thing I remember after that was the image lit with sunlight and feeling the world fade away around me as I slumped to the floor.

Chapter 8

Now I realized I was lying on the floor of what would soon be my bedroom, my head on something soft. What the hell happened? Then I remembered what I'd seen.

I looked up quizzically. Tom was kneeling beside me, his eyes unmistakably concerned. I tried to sit up, but he kept a firm hand on my shoulder. "Stay still, Lily. My mom is on her way to check you out."

"Your mom?"

He tried to smile. "She's an RN. She's coming up because you fainted."

I tried again to sit up, realizing that someone had grabbed a pillow from the couch downstairs, and it was tucked under my head. "I'm fine, Tom. Let me up."

My stubborn streak seemed to amuse him. "Nice to see you still have your fire, but no, you aren't getting up.

50

You are going to stay right here until she checks you out. I will sit on you if I have to."

His voice had the tone my mom used to use when there was no use arguing with her. I rolled my eyes but laid back on the pillow, closing them finally, so I couldn't see the worried look on Tom's face.

Ten minutes later, an older woman I assumed to be Tom's mom bustled into the room with a little boy right behind her. "Lily," she said, "I'm Gladys. I'm sorry we are meeting under these circumstances." She glanced at her son. "You did good, Tommy. Now take Jake and go do something while I give Lily a once-over."

Tom squeezed my hand. "I better do what she says."

The man who'd ordered me to stay still was gone, and in his place was a son who was listening to his mother. That made me smile. "You better."

Once Tom and Jake left the room, Gladys helped me sit up, placing a steady hand on my back. Then she asked me a million questions, checked my eyes and how they responded to light, and finally deemed me concussion-free. She helped me to my feet and guided me to the window seat. She sat and looked at me; her expression was serious. "So, what made you faint? Did you eat today?"

"I did."

"Any issues with blood pressure?"

"No."

"Any chance you're pregnant?"

I chuckled. "Not a chance."

"That was rather definitive." She patted my hand. "When was your last physical?"

The look on my face must have given my answer away. "Then, kiddo, you need to get a physical. There is a great woman doctor in town. She's down-to-earth and swears like a sailor but she loves to laugh and she's brilliant. Get checked out, okay?"

I knew exactly why I had fainted, but since I had never fainted before, it probably was a good idea to make sure I was okay. After all, I had been shocked before and never had that physical reaction. "I will," I said. "I promise."

We found Tom and his crew stripping wallpaper downstairs in what had been the formal parlor. Jake was helping them by carrying pieces over to the debris pile. When I came through the door, he looked up at me joyfully. "Daddy, she's okay. Look, she's with Grandma."

Tom ruffled the little boy's curly blond hair and smiled. "She is, buddy. Come on over here, please." Leading the boy by the hand, Tom brought him over to me. "Lily, this is my son Jacob, or Jake. Jake, this is Ms. Brannan."

The boy held a small hand out to shake mine, and I was immediately smitten with his bright blue eyes, blond curls, and the freckles that had been sprinkled across his nose. "Hi, Jake." I shook his hand seriously. "If it's okay with your daddy, you can call me Lily."

He gazed up at Tom quizzically, and Tom nodded. Jake's smile was immediate. "Hi, Lily."

Tom turned to his mother. "She's okay?"

I glared. "*She* is right here, you know."

He ignored me. "Mom?"

Gladys laughed. "Lily is fine. She's going to make an appointment for a physical, but that's it. She's good to go for today, although she should take it easy for the rest of the day just to be sure."

Just then, there was a knock on the front door. Who the hell could that be? Other than Berto, everyone I knew in the area was already in the room with me. "Excuse me, I'll see who's at the door."

Berto was standing on the front porch, and he did not look happy. I put on a pleased expression and opened the door. "Berto," I said breezily, "I wasn't expecting you."

"I gather that." He threw a glance over my shoulder. "Looks like you have quite a group here already."

I did not like his tone, although I could not put my finger on why. "Berto, that's the work crew. And Tom's mother is here too."

"Why?"

"Why, what?"

"Why is his mother here?" Somehow, again today, Berto's questions rubbed me the wrong way. They weren't coming off as concerned, more as controlling.

Maybe they weren't. Maybe the shock was making me hear things a certain way. Could that be it?

"Lily, I asked you a question!"

I sighed. I would have preferred to keep the whole fainting thing to myself; I felt stupid. "Because I fainted a while ago and she's a nurse, so Tom had her check on me."

"You fainted and you didn't let me know?" Now his tone was full-out accusatory.

"Berto," I snapped, "it literally just happened, and I'm fine. Now, tell me, what's up? Why did you come up?"

"Because I've been trying to reach you since mid-morning, that's why. When I didn't hear from you, I got worried." He gestured with his hand. "I don't like you living so far out of town, up here all alone. You should put the house on the market and move to civilization."

I ignored his comments. "Berto, thank you for worrying about me. I must have left my ringer off this morning. I was in the writing zone, and when that happens, I miss it completely if the sound is off." I stretched up to kiss his cheek. "Thank you, and I'm sorry for worrying you." Was I really sorry, or was I just trying to placate him? I'd need to figure that out, but not right now.

He stroked my cheek, his hand warm against my skin. "Okay, my bella, I'm sorry for seeming so cross."

"It's okay." I took his hand. "Want to come in and see the progress?"

He shook his head. "I would love to, my darling, but I need to get back for my next class." He checked his watch. "I need to hurry. Dinner tonight?"

I shook my head. "Thank you for the invitation, but I think I'm going to have an early night. I should get some extra sleep after today's excitement."

He pursed his lips, clearly irritated, but his tone had returned to normal. "I understand," he said. "Tomorrow then?"

Did I want to commit to having dinner with him tomorrow? At that moment, I didn't know. "I'll give you a call in the morning and let you know."

That clearly wasn't the answer he wanted or expected, and his face tightened, but his voice was gentle. "Good. Sleep well, and please, my love, please think about what I said. Put this place on the market and move to town. Please." His eyes were warm. "All I want is to know you are safe."

"Thank you, Berto." I squeezed his hand. "I'll talk to you in the morning."

There was no way in hell I was giving up this house, especially after finding that window, but I was not going to tell him that.

Chapter 9

I watched Berto drive slowly down the hill. Something was off, but I could not figure out what it was. He had come all this way to check on me, which was really sweet, but then he turned around and left as soon as he arrived. If he was so worried, why didn't he cancel his class, or at least have his TA step in to teach? Couldn't he have stayed for ten more minutes?

And why was he so hot on the idea that I sell the house? Shit, we weren't even sleeping together—why did he care where I lived? Was he simply worried about my safety up here? Furthermore, why was our relationship still relegated to dinners out, walks, and phone calls? He claimed to be attracted to me, but seriously, I've had bigger reactions to paint samples. Shit. He called me darling, his *bella*, his love, but other than a few kisses, what did we have when things seemed to be going nowhere?

I had to wonder if I was turning him off in some way. He was gorgeous, elegant, and refined, but after this amount of time, it was logical to expect some passionate exchanges. I'd never had to work this hard before to get a man to touch me. Hell, I'd even tried to touch him, and he'd rebuffed me, claiming it was too soon. Why didn't he want me to go to his place or spend time at mine?

I shook my head, then felt silly as I realized I had just rattled all my concerns off out loud. I really needed to remember I was not alone anymore, at least for now. I needed to work on keeping the running commentary in my head, where it belonged, instead of talking to myself like I'd done for the last several years of living alone.

I heard a noise and turned to see Tom standing in the doorway. Mortification filled me. "You just heard all of that, didn't you?"

He nodded and squirmed. "Sorry, Lily, I didn't mean to eavesdrop. When you didn't come back inside, I wanted to be sure you were okay." He looked down at his feet to avoid my eyes. "I have to admit, you gave me a scare when you fainted."

Somehow, Tom's worry made me feel warm and squishy inside, and yet I had been irritated with Berto for the same thing. What the hell was wrong with me? I smiled. "Thanks," I said, "I appreciate it. And yes, I'm a fricking mess. Anything you heard me mumbling... Well, please pretend you didn't hear it."

"Deal."

The rest of the afternoon was uneventful. Jake left with Gladys after giving me at least five hugs. Those little kid hugs were awesome; I felt like the queen of the world when he told me he was going to come back soon, as he had plans to color a picture for my office.

Speaking of my office, I was back there working when I heard several of the trucks leave at the end of the day. Tom knocked on my open door. "Hi," he said.

"Hey."

Clearly, something was on his mind. "What's up?"

"Are you okay?"

"What do you mean?"

"Look, I know we agreed to forget that I heard you talking to yourself, but it sounded like you've got a lot on your mind. And I know something about that stained glass upset you, causing you to faint. Do you want to talk about it?"

I closed my laptop and gazed at him for a moment. The thing was, I liked Tom. Yes, I knew I was paying him a lot of money to renovate the house, and that was the only reason we had met, but still, I liked him. He was smart, funny, and kind, and he didn't seem to think I was crazy when I got into writing mode. He was as close to a friend as anyone I had in Vermont. "Want a beer?"

He smiled. "Sure."

I got up and walked past him into the kitchen, grabbed two beers, and handed one to him. Before I could open my own, he twisted the top off his and handed it back to me. "Here. Give me that one."

I took it. "Thanks." I sat on a kitchen stool, waiting while he did the same. "I am out of my element here."

"What do you mean?"

"Shit, Tom, since my mom died, I've either lived in cities or at school. Then I inherited this place, which I love, but I still have no fucking idea why the old bat had it and why she left it to me. I had never even heard of this place until the day her will was read."

Tom put up a hand. "Okay, Lily. Wait. I have no idea what you're talking about."

I put my head in my hands, suddenly feeling very tired. "How much time do you have?"

He laughed. "All the time you need."

"What about Jake?"

"Every Friday he goes out to dinner with my mom at the Five Guys in St. Johnsbury, then they go grocery shopping, and he has a sleepover at her house. It originally started when he was a baby, so I could get one full night of sleep a week, but now it's their special time. So, take your time, I've got all the time you want. Tell me what you want to share with me."

"Want to stay for dinner?" I felt nervous asking. "I was going to grill a steak and I have plenty."

"I'd love to."

"Then how about we get dinner going, and I'll explain it all."

"Sounds good."

We worked in companionable silence, Tom making a salad while I put potatoes in to bake, then prepped the steak for the grill. I wrapped a mini baguette in foil to heat while the steak cooked.

"I think we've done all we can for now." Tom opened a bottle of red wine and poured two glasses. "Ready to talk?"

Somehow, I was very ready to talk. "I am," I said. "Have a seat."

We both sat. I took a deep breath. "So, my mother was seventeen when she had me."

He nodded. "Okay."

"My mom..." I swallowed. God, I missed her so much, even after all these years. "Her name was Kathryn, Katie. She raised me by herself. She was amazing. She got her GED, went to community college to get her degree, and always made sure I felt loved."

"Wow."

"Yeah. It was just the two of us. I never knew my father; she wouldn't tell me who he was." I took a sip. "She was a good mom. We were poor, which I later realized was not her fault."

"What do you mean?"

"She came from a lot of money. I mean, a lot. My grandmother was dead, and my grandfather disowned her when she got pregnant. He told her to either get an abortion or give me up for adoption, or he would cut her off." I smiled, suddenly proud. "She told him to fuck off, and she walked away from everything."

"I'm impressed."

"Me too. She had me in a women's shelter in Albany, New York, then moved here to Vermont. We lived in Rutland, then Burlington, then Whiting. She worked; she took care of us. We had a good life together."

"Good."

Suddenly my eyes filled with tears. "Mom got sick when I was eleven; she had breast cancer. She fought it for two years but died when I was thirteen."

He reached out and put his hand over mine, squeezing it comfortingly. "I am so sorry."

"Me too. I still miss her every day." I sniffed back the tears. "Then my grandfather died too, not knowing she'd died, and he left everything to my mom."

"Shit."

"Yup." I wiped a lingering tear. "I was suddenly an orphan, and my only living relative was my great-aunt Helen, my grandfather's sister. She had guardianship of me."

"And?"

I laughed, but more out of irony than amusement. "Even if she liked you, she was a bitch. But me? She hated me. My mother died on a Saturday, and her funeral was one week later. Just two days after that I was sent to Ms. Porter's School for Girls. She saw me as an embarrassment to the family name, so she sent me away as quickly as she could." I swallowed hard, remembering my shame. "The headmistress told me that she'd paid extra to have me start mid-semester because she wanted me there as soon as possible."

His voice cracked with anger. "You're kidding me."

"I wish I was. I was shipped off to boarding school, and Helen even arranged for me to remain there for the summer session. I was thirteen, and for the most part, I stayed there until I graduated high school, aside from the few weeks I was permitted home… if you want to call it that. Before leaving for college, I was sent to a prep camp—her way of not having to deal with me, I suppose. She hated me."

"Jesus."

"My grandfather's estate had been put into a trust fund; Helen could only touch it to pay my expenses. After that, I inherited everything when I turned twenty-five. By then, I had graduated college, gotten married, and become a writer. When I got divorced, I just kept going on with my life. I saw Helen for about an hour, once a year, but that was it. I'd show up, she'd tell me all the things I'd done wrong or was doing wrong, according to her rules of life. I'd bite my tongue, try to just shut up, have a great time visiting her wonderful housekeeper, then leave."

Tom's face showed his sadness. "I am so sorry, Lily. What a horrible way to be treated."

I continued. "Then a couple of months ago, Helen died and left me nearly everything. Not because she wanted to, or because she liked me, but because she hated most other people. She left it to me because she hated me the least."

"Wow."

"But I had no idea this house existed. For years, she held her damn will over my head, so I was pretty familiar with what was coming to me. This house was a complete surprise, and I still don't have any idea why it was left to me, or frankly, why the hell she had it, since she never once mentioned it."

"And no one can tell you?"

"Not so far." I stood up. "Okay, enough for now. Let's get on with dinner."

We finished the dinner preparations, and I set the table. I picked up the bottle of wine and refilled our glasses. "Cheers," I said.

"Cheers." Tom nodded.

As I ate, I snuck glances at Tom. What was I doing drinking wine and spilling my guts to this gorgeous man? I'd shared more with him tonight than I'd ever shared with anyone other than my now ex-husband and my best friend, and certainly, more than I'd told Berto. What was I doing?

Chapter 10

I cut a small piece of steak and popped it in my mouth. "Okay, so..."

He chuckled. "This is great, thank you."

"You're welcome."

He took a sip, then asked, "Is it okay if I ask questions?"

"Of course." Jesus, after what I'd already shared, why would he think he needed to ask that?

"What happened with your marriage?"

I laughed. "Well, that is a hell of a story."

"Want to tell it?"

Why not? In for a penny, in for a pound. "Sure. I met my now ex-husband David in college. We got married the day after we graduated and he became not only my husband, but my writing partner too. I thought our marriage would be perfect."

"And clearly, it wasn't."

"In many ways it was. I mean, we still are business partners. But, well, my husband..." Shit, this was awkward. "My husband wanted to have an open marriage," I blurted.

Tom's shock was clear. "Seriously? How open? And does that mean what I think it does?"

"Yes." I took a sip. "To be specific, he wanted an open marriage so he could also be with my college roommate, my best friend Megan."

"Ew." Tom looked embarrassed. "Sorry, that's just my gut reaction."

I laughed. "It was mine too. So, he wanted this, she wanted this, and I didn't."

"And?"

"He tried to fight his feelings; we went to counseling, but we finally had to admit it wasn't going to work, so we divorced." I shook my head. "He married my roommate two days after our divorce was finalized, and they are now in a fully open marriage."

"Really?"

"Yeah." I closed my eyes, wanting to tell him the rest, but I knew I couldn't look at him as I did. "She has three lovers outside of their marriage, that I know about anyway, and he has two. Or did. And, in the interest of being completely honest, I was one of them until I came up here."

I opened my eyes to look at Tom. He was silent for a few seconds, then he smiled. "Well, that had to be hard to say."

"It was."

"And why did it end when you came here?"

That was a great question. I had not thought of it as officially over until this conversation. Somehow, in talking about it, I realized that part of my life was over. "I don't really know," I said. "David is still my writing partner; Megan is still my best friend. But coming back to Vermont has made me realize I need to simplify my life. It worked for a while, but not anymore."

"Okay." He reached out to touch my hand. "I'm not judging, Lily. Really, I'm not. Yes, I did judge your ex for wanting an open marriage, but your part after? That was between the two of you."

"Thanks."

"So, that's your divorce and writing career. What about coming here and meeting Roberto?"

"I first met him at the pizza place, and we started going out. But as you probably heard me muttering about on the porch, things seem to have stalled and I don't know why."

"What do you mean?"

I picked up the bottle of wine and realized it was empty. "Want more?"

"Sure."

I grabbed another bottle and handed it to him with the corkscrew. "Will you open it?"

"Of course." He did it quickly and refilled the glasses. "Here you go."

"Thanks." I turned the glass around in my hands, admiring the deep color of the wine. "I guess before Berto, I was pretty secure in my looks. Yes, my husband wanted to sleep with other women, but he also still wanted me. I thought I was attractive, but Berto is keeping the physicality to an absolute minimum. All of our dates have been in public, he barely kisses me, and when I've invited him over, he turns me down."

"Really?"

"Yeah, he says he cares about me too much to rush things. I don't think it's rushing to expect something beyond light kissing after two months."

Tom was silent, which suddenly irritated me. "What? No response to that?"

Tom held up his hands in surrender. "Look, Lily, I have strong opinions about him. I'm letting you tell your story and I'm doing my best to keep my thoughts on the matter to myself."

"What do you mean, you have strong opinions about him?"

Tom took a deep breath. "Look, when he moved here, I did some work for him. He was seriously the biggest pain in the ass I have ever encountered. He was downright nasty. He didn't pay his bills on time, and when he did, his checks bounced. Not to mention I found him to be condescending."

Somehow, this did not surprise me. I could see Berto being difficult to someone he saw as *just* a tradesman. "Oh," I said. "I guess I can see him doing that. He does have a snobbish side."

"Beyond that, he dated a girl I went to high school with, and I can tell you, he didn't have the same reservations about getting physical with her."

That didn't exactly make me feel awesome. As soon as he finished the statement, Tom saw the look on my face. "Oh, Lily. Shit, I didn't mean to hurt your feelings. I am so sorry."

I sighed. "Well, it did, but I know you didn't mean to, so it's okay. It just puts things into perspective. I knew something was off, so I guess I should thank you for just plain saying it instead of keeping it to yourself."

"What are you going to do about it?"

I shrugged. "I don't know. I guess I need to figure out if I care enough to talk to him about it. If not, I need to step back from him. If I do decide to confront him, I need to sit down and have a brutally honest conversation with him."

"Okay."

"Let's clean up," I said.

He smiled. "You mean before you tell me why the window upset you so much?"

"That's exactly what I mean."

Chapter 11

I washed, and Tom dried. When the kitchen was
sparkling again, I turned to lean against the counter. "So,
before we talk about the window, tell me your story."

"Sure."

We sat back down at the counter. He shrugged.
"What do you want to know?"

"How did your dad die?"

"Heart attack. He was a lawyer in town, and in
hindsight, he didn't take great care of himself."

"I'm sorry."

"Me too. Mom raised us on her own. She worked as
a school nurse, then also worked extra shifts at the
hospital in the ER. It wasn't easy, but she kept us all
together, and like your mom, she made sure we always
knew we were loved."

"That was clear when I met her."

72

"It is."

I had to ask the question that had been swirling around in my mind a lot lately. "And no marriages for you?"

"No." A flash of pain crossed his face. "I was engaged at the time my brother died. She left when I said I was going to adopt Jake."

Ouch. I couldn't imagine doing that, especially right after Tom had also lost his brother. "Shit."

"Yeah. But at least I can say I'm glad it happened before we got married. It made it simpler."

"And you always wanted to be a contractor?"

"No." He took a sip of his wine. "I went to college to be an architect."

That surprised me. "Really?"

"What, someone who bangs nails can't be educated?"

Shit, I had hit a nerve. "I didn't mean it that way, Tom. I'm sorry."

"Me too. That's a hot button for me."

"So, tell me about the architect thing."

"I trained as an architect, and actually, I'm still licensed as one. But I liked building things more than planning them, so I made the move to construction and design. For years, my business grew and grew, and the projects were getting bigger and bigger, and I was on the road constantly. Since Jake, I decided to focus on more local projects, so I am always available for him."

"That's really cool. Do you ever miss working on bigger projects?"

"No. Too many people get involved, and I can't control the quality as well as I can on a smaller project."

"Like this one."

"Exactly."

It was time to tell him. "I need to show you something," I said.

"Okay."

"Do you remember what that stained glass window looked like?"

He looked at me like I had lost my mind, which maybe I had. "Of course," he said.

I was dressed in my normal writing uniform – leggings and a fitted tank topped by a loose sweater. I stood and turned my back to Tom, dropping the sweater off my right shoulder so he could see the tattoo there.

I heard him gasp. "Holy fuck."

The stool creaked as he pushed it back to stand up. His finger was gentle as he traced the black lines I knew so well. "How...?"

"I don't know." I dropped my shoulders and felt unexpected tears welling up. "I don't know, Tom. I really have no clue how this happened."

My voice must have told him how distressed I was because before I knew what was happening, he was adjusting my sweater back up over my shoulder, turning me around, and pulling me into his arms. His touch was gentle and comforting as he hugged me. "It's okay, Lily. We'll figure it out."

I started to cry. Here I was, in the middle of Nowhere, Vermont, in a house that had been given to me for God-only-knew-what reason, in a relationship with a truly odd man, attracted to the man holding me, and my body was permanently marked with a unique tattoo that somehow exactly matched the mysterious window that had been discovered upstairs.

Tom's tone was soothing. "Shh, Lily. Don't cry, sweetie. It's okay."

Finally, I knew I had to step out of his arms. Being that close to him was bringing my already overeager hormones raging to the surface, and I had to move away before I did something stupid. He had given no hint that he found me attractive, so I needed to stuff down anything I was wanting in that moment. "Let's go look at the window again," I said.

We held hands as we walked upstairs like I remembered doing on walks with my mom when I was a child. The window was still leaning against the wall of my future bedroom. The window was large; it must have originally been in the large window space at the top of the main staircase. Even without the sun shining through the somewhat dusty glass, the colors were deep and beautiful. The solid black lines gave the outline of a tree, with the colored glass filling in the outline. It was stunning, so new to me, and yet, so familiar.

My shock was still bubbling but not as strong now as the confusion and desire to understand grew. "I don't get it. Why is it here, and why was it hidden?"

Tom knelt for a closer look, and I did the same. "I don't know," he said. "But it was carefully placed in that wall. It looked like someone had slid it in there to protect it, and the only place I can see where that could have happened is where one piece of window trim doesn't match the others. I think whoever put it here removed the trim, slid it in the wall, then replaced the trim."

"But why?"

"I don't know." He reached out to put a hand over my shoulder, where the tattoo was now hidden. I could feel the warmth of his hand through my sweater, and it was comforting. "How did you decide on the design for the tattoo?"

It was going to sound crazy; I knew that. "I had a dream about it," I said. "Several actually. They started when I was about seventeen. I could see the design so clearly, and finally I drew it out from memory. When I turned eighteen, I got the tattoo."

"Could you have seen it before? The window, I mean."

"I don't think so, but maybe. I don't remember seeing it, that's for sure."

He stood back up and pulled me to my feet. "Then we have a mystery on our hands," he said.

That sounded funny to me, and it made me giggle. "I might have to write a book about it; I've never written a mystery before."

"Sounds like it may be a good time to start."

Chapter 12

Once we were downstairs, Tom looked at me. "Okay, I should head out."

"Really?"

He smiled. "Really."

"You don't have to go."

His eyes were dark and warm as he looked down at me, then reached out to stroke my cheek with the back of his hand. The touch shot a bolt of electricity through me. This was not the platonic kind of touch. I closed my eyes for a split second, chastising myself. I was making things up. He had touched me several times that day, and none of it had been sexual. I was just imagining things now.

There was a small smile on his lips. "No, you're not wrong," he said.

"What?"

"I just felt that too." He moved his hand slowly on my face, causing me to take in a sharp breath. Damn, that was *hot*. "And it's time for me to go," he said.

How could he leave now after what we'd both just felt? Why were men turning me down left and right recently? "Why?"

His posture changed, and his other hand came up to cradle my face. "Let me be clear, Lily. We both just felt that. That was the desire I've been trying to ignore since the moment I first saw you. You are the cause of me needing a cold shower every single day now." Okay, that made me almost swoon with the power of my arousal. He did want me! He continued, "But I don't share well. Never did if you believe my mother. And it seems there are two other men in your life who have dibs before me."

Was that true? I started to argue. "But..."

"But nothing. If you were mine, I would never be looking for anyone else in my bed, unlike your ex. And as for Berto? He's a fucking idiot if he loses you. You are offering yourself to the man and he seems to be putting up roadblocks."

I needed to make him understand. "This isn't about either of them, it's about you and me."

"No, Lily. It can't be about you and me until they aren't involved." His thumb gently stroked my bottom lip, and I could feel my knees go weak. "I'll say it again... I don't share."

I stood there, unsure of what to do or say next. "Please."

"There is no need for please, Lily. Get them out of your life in that way, and I'll be here in a second." With that, he leaned down and kissed me.

The second his lips touched mine, I swear I felt the floor fall away under my feet. It was like no other kiss in my life. I felt my heart grow like the stupid Grinch, and my body was immediately engulfed in heat, ready for him as I had never been before for any other man.

He pulled back. "That is our last kiss unless it's just us."

Fuck! That was not what I wanted to hear. What I wanted to hear was that he was staying the night, letting me finally explore his amazing body. But, no. He was leaving. Shit!

He opened the door. "Goodnight, Lily. Thanks for dinner, I'll see you on Monday."

Two hours later, I was trying to focus on a movie after failing miserably at writing. I slid under the covers on my pullout couch. What a mind-fuck! The window, Berto's odd behavior, and then Tom.

I lay in bed and contemplated my life. What did I want? Who did I want?

Berto was charming, handsome, and urbane. We could talk about cities of the world and opera. I loved his European mannerisms. He was fascinated by my writing career and seemed like he had no issue with me needing time on my own to write. That was a plus.

But he hated this house, and every second I was here, I was more in love with the place. Could he get over that?

Then there was David. Well, not really. David would always be my writing partner, that was certain, but did I want him in my bed anymore? He was great in bed, always had been, but was it time to step away from that completely, and like, tell him it was done? And could I really keep that promise if I made it?

And now, there was Tom. How the hell had we gone from just buddies to kissing like that? Let's face it, I thought he was attractive right from the start, too, but it seemed like he wasn't interested. Now, what was I supposed to do?

Berto was moving too slowly. Tom wasn't moving at all.

Berto came with a life of refinement. Tom came with a kid.

I snorted as I realized I was talking to myself again. With a growl, I rolled over and pulled the covers up to my ears and told myself to go to sleep.

Yeah, right. I wasn't going to get much sleep, that was for sure.

Chapter 13

The next morning, I climbed out of bed as soon as the sun began to peek through my windows. I slept fitfully, with dreams of the stained glass interspersed with snippets of memories with David and Berto, and fantasies of Tom.

I started my day in a foul mood. As I stood up, I stepped on the pen I had been using to edit the night before, which hurt like hell and elicited an epic rant of profanity.

I limped into the kitchen and flipped the coffeemaker on. Thankfully, I had remembered to set it up the night before, so it was all ready. Thank God for small victories, I thought, as there is nothing that makes me crankier than to have to set up for coffee in the morning when I'm all ready for my first jolt of caffeine.

I kept a stash of mini donuts in the freezer for times when I couldn't force myself to eat like a responsible adult, and that was what this morning called for. I pulled them out, popped them into the microwave, and got the iPad, so I could check the forecast and the news.

Just then, my phone lit up with a text. *Bella, how about joining me for breakfast at the diner this morning?*

That was just what I needed, I thought as I rolled my eyes. *Thanks for the invitation, but I got up early to write, and I have already eaten.*

It was several minutes before he responded. *Are you angry with me?*

Why? Should I be? As soon as I hit send, I regretted that message. After all, my confusion was not his fault.

Is there something going on? Have I done something to upset you?

It was time to stop texting like I was a teenager. I hit call and waited for him to answer.

"Lily. Good morning."

"Hi, Berto."

"Are you okay, *bella*? You seem upset with me." He sounded forlorn.

I tried to reign in my emotions. "Oh, Berto, I'm not upset; I just don't understand where we are in terms of us."

"What do you mean?" Now he sounded confused. How could he be confused about this?

"You say you care about me, and you seem to, but we only go out in public. Our physical relationship is nonexistent. You hate my house. You tell me you don't want me to live here. I don't get it." I paused. "Then there was yesterday. You came up here, saying you were so worried, but you didn't even stay for five minutes. I don't understand what you want from us as a couple. I'm completely confused."

"*Bella*, listen to me. I am crazy about you. Probably too crazy. You are all I can think of, and I don't want to waste my love for you on a fling."

Love? Did he just say his *love* for me? Holy fuck. That was a whole different ball game, and I didn't know how I felt about it.

He was still talking. "And darling, you are too special to me for us to just jump into bed together. I've done that before; I don't want to do that with you."

Well, shit… How did I respond to that comment? "Oh."

He lowered his voice, and it was like a caress in my ear. "Lily, I am in love with you. You are my life. I am sorry if I haven't expressed that to you in the right way, my love. If I have not shown you how much I love you and made you secure in that love, that is on me. I have failed. Please, my love, please let me show you how much I love you."

Wow.

Whoa.

Wait a minute.

My lack of sleep, combined with swirling emotions and Berto's confession, was making my head spin. "Berto. Wow. This is a lot to take in. Please understand that I'm overwhelmed."

His voice changed to one of slight irritation. "How can hearing that the man you are with loves you be overwhelming? Don't you love me?"

The question took me by surprise, although maybe it shouldn't have. Most people automatically respond to such a statement with "I love you, too."

Did I love Berto? It struck me that I didn't know him well enough to know if I loved him. Our relationship had been so short and limited in scope that I couldn't say I loved him, but I also couldn't say I didn't.

I sighed, but he cut me off before I could say a word. "The fact that you haven't answered tells me you either don't love me and don't want to hurt me, or you have doubts that my feelings are true."

"Berto, I'm just stunned. That visit bothered me yesterday. I was doubting what I meant to you, and frankly, I was beginning to think we shouldn't be together. Now, given this conversation, I need to think. I need to absorb what you've said and see how I feel."

He was silent, so I continued. "Please, Berto, if you really love me, I need time. Please give me the time to think about this, about us."

I waited for him to speak, and finally, I heard him clear his throat. "Lily, of course. I hoped you felt as strongly as I do, but I understand if I haven't made my feelings clear to you, that this might surprise you."

"Thank you."

"Could we have dinner here together tomorrow night? To talk?"

"Here?"

"Here, darling, at my house."

At his place? Wow. That was a big step. Then I remembered my schedule. "I have a Zoom meeting tomorrow night that is likely to take several hours. Remember? I told you about it; it's with the editor and graphic designer."

"Of course, I do remember now. Would Monday work?" His voice grew silky. "It seems like forever from now, but for you, I will do anything."

"Monday it is," I said. "I'll see you then."

"I love you, my darling."

I hung up the phone and stared at the dark screen. What the hell had just happened? How did I go from thinking this guy really wasn't into me to him professing his love? And how did I know if I loved him back?

There was only one way to figure this out. It was time to call the two people on earth who knew me better than anyone else. I picked up my phone to call David and Megan.

Chapter 14

David answered on the third ring, and from his voice, I knew I woke him. "Hey, it's me. Sorry for waking you up, but I need you guys."

"Hold on," he growled. "Meg, wake up. Lily needs us." He paused. "I'm putting you on speaker."

Megan's voice came on the line. "You okay?"

"Yeah, but I need the two of you to help me think something through."

Meg immediately morphed into her professional lawyer role. "Okay, go."

"I met this guy Roberto Romano, Berto, here in Vermont. Hot Italian, very Euro, smart, sexy, kind of over the top in terms of manner and dress, but amazing."

"Okay."

"And?" (That was David.)

"It just happens that I fainted yesterday, and he showed up at my house not long after because he was worried that I didn't answer my phone. But he only stayed for a couple minutes."

"Are you okay?" Megan asked.

"Yes, I'm fine." I took a breath. "Long story short, he was kind of a jerk. Then my contractor, Tom, stayed for dinner and I told him about my life, about all of us, and talked about my tattoo."

"What about your tattoo?" David sounded awake now. "Why is that even part of the story?"

That's an editor for you; I'm telling a personal story, and he wants to cut out useless dialogue. "David," I exclaimed, "shut up and listen. Yesterday, the crew found a stained-glass window hidden in a wall, and it has the exact same design as my tattoo."

"Fuck." David sounded rattled. "Shit, Lily, you had dreams for months about that design. What the hell is that all about?"

"I don't know," I yelled. "I told Tom everything, and well, then we kissed, and it was amazing. But he told me that absolutely nothing, and I mean nothing, will happen between us until I'm done with Berto, and I end the sex thing with you, David."

"Wow. Okay. Continue." David sniffed, a sign that he was getting angry or possessive or both. "We'll talk about that later."

"I spent the night trying to sort this all out, and then I just talked to Berto and he told me he loves me and wants to be with me, like, seriously."

Megan chuckled. "Well, that's sure an interesting start to the day."

"What do I do?" I wailed.

There was silence. Then David cleared his throat. "Lily, since you didn't say you told him you loved him too, I assume you do not echo the sentiment."

"Correct. Well, I have no frigging clue if I do. I don't think I know him enough to know that. I mean, I don't know if he steals the covers. I don't know if he leaves his socks on the bathroom floor. I don't know if he puts the jelly knife into the peanut butter jar. How can I know if I love him if I don't know those things about him?"

Megan chuckled. "It's amazing that David does all of those things, but they didn't bother you at first."

"I know." I felt defeated. "What do I do?"

David's voice was gentle. "Lily, if you don't know enough about him to know if you love him, then you could always try getting to know him better. On the other side of the coin, if you were kissing Tom last night, you could walk away from Berto and see what happens with Tom."

Megan interrupted. "As a third choice, you could put them both on hold and take some time for yourself to see who you miss or think about more."

That sounded like a good idea. Then it hit me. "I can't really do that, at least with Tom. He's renovating the house. We see each other constantly."

David yawned. "It's too early to be thinking this hard, Lil. If you can't avoid him there, then take a break for a couple days. Come down here and stay with us. Go to Montreal or something."

Montreal? That was an idea I hadn't considered, and that sounded really good. "I could go to Old Montreal, stay in a hotel, sleep late, order room service, and think."

Megan laughed. "And shop, get a pedicure, shit like that. Hell, Lily, it would do you a world of good."

It would, indeed.

Chapter 15

I opened my laptop. Within ten minutes, I had a reservation at a lovely hotel I knew in Old Montreal. I was going on a trip. Just me, for no reason other than to think, and it was going to be glorious.

I was going to take some time for absolute self-care and reflection and figure out what I wanted in my life. No, I was going to figure out *who* I wanted in my life and how.

I was to leave that afternoon, driving straight there to be at the hotel by dinner. I was going to do the call with my publisher from Montreal and then take a couple of days completely off from the world.

Packing was simple. I wasn't trying to impress anyone. But Megan was right; maybe I would do some shopping while I was there.

I took my shower, dressed for driving such a distance, then went back down to my office. I packed my laptop and tablet and the other necessities to work remotely. I was ready to go.

Shit, there was one more thing, well, two, that I needed to do before leaving. I had to tell Tom and Berto. Call? Text? Email? What was the right way to say, "I need to get the hell away from you both to get my head on straight"?

Texting was the easiest.

Berto, after our talk this morning, I realized I need some time to be alone and think. I'm going away for a few days, until at least Wednesday. I will call you as soon as I get back, but I am shutting my phone off for a few days.

Just then, my phone pinged. It was a text from Tom. *Hi, Lily. I just wanted to apologize for how I acted last night and to say I'm going to take a few days off from your project. The guys will be there, but I think I need to step away for a bit. Text me if you need something.*

Interesting. I texted back. *Hi, your text made me smile because I was just texting you to say that I was going away for a few days to get my head on straight. I should be back on Thursday or so. I will let you know when I return.*

Ding. A text from Berto. *Love, please don't go away. Let's think this out together. I love you enough for both of us. Stay and let me show you how much I love you.*

Ding. Tom. *Safe travels and clear thinking.*

Did I need to respond to Berto? I had told him I was shutting my phone off. Fuck. I slowly typed. *Thanks for believing in me and in us, but I do need to take this time. See you later in the week.*

I turned notifications off on my phone. I was going to take care of myself, and I was going to take a break. Period.

Aside from a long line of traffic at the border crossing, the drive was uneventful. I had only crossed into Canada once before by car, and that had been at the big crossing north of Burlington. This was a tiny crossing, and it took forever.

Once through the border, it was smooth sailing, and I was in Montreal more than an hour earlier than I had expected. Handing my keys over to the valet, I was escorted to my luxury suite in what seemed like only minutes.

The rooms were gorgeous. Old brick walls, windows looking out at the city, and a chilled bottle of white wine waiting for me. I picked up the card with interest. Only David and Megan, and my agent knew where I was. The note was short: *Sleep, drink, eat, go to the spa, and the answer will come to you. We love you - D and M.*

With that, I opened the wine and poured myself a glass. That was exactly what I needed. I reached for the room phone and called the front desk. "Hello, this is room five-nineteen. I need a room service menu and information about booking with the hotel spa."

On Thursday morning, I handed the valet a hefty tip as he relinquished my keys. I had slept late every day, eaten my favorite foods, gotten my hair cut, and had a manicure, pedicure, and massage. And, yes, I had spent too many hours weighing how I felt about Berto, and what I wanted to do there, and if Tom factored into any of this. I had reached my decision. I was ready to head home.

The trip home was a breeze until I hit the border and had to sit and wait. With a sigh, I reached for my phone and turned the notifications back on.

It was like a tidal wave had hit my phone. Berto had texted me at least five times each day, all with declarations of love and devotion. At first, I felt a swell of sweet emotion, then, I admit, I was irritated. Stop being so needy, I groaned.

Then, yesterday, and today, there were several messages from Tom. Those weren't declarations of love but pronouncements of having to talk to me about the house and the urgency of calling back.

The last one was pretty decisive; it was short. *Lily, I need you to call me NOW. We need to tell you what is going on here. I don't know how long I can keep this under wraps.*

Chapter 16

What the hell did that message mean? I waited to cross the border, then hit speed dial for Tom's number. Berto could wait. Five rings, then the voicemail kicked in. I grimaced. "Tom, it's Lily. I just got your messages. I just crossed the border, heading home. Call me, please."

I drove faster than I should. What was going on at my house? I felt both fear and anticipation.

Finally, the familiar landmarks started coming into view. I was almost home. What was I going to find?

Just then, my phone rang. It was Berto. "Hi," I said.

"Hello, darling. Where are you?"

"I am about a half hour from home. Almost there. I will probably lose the signal any moment now, but I will call you when I arrive and get settled."

"Oh, Lily, that sounds so good. I have missed you so much. My love, I will see you this evening, yes?"

This was my decision. Berto was my boyfriend, and I wanted to see what was going to happen with him. "Yes, please, Berto. Would you come to my house for dinner tonight?"

"Love, I will go anywhere to see you. Does seven work? Would you like me to cook for you?"

"I'm happy to cook. Seven works."

Pulling into my driveway, Tom's crew vehicles were all there, as well as his truck. Why was everyone here?

Suddenly, my heart jumped. Berto's car was there too. What the hell was going on?

I jumped out of the car, leaving everything behind. I could unpack later. I jogged up the front steps and pushed the door open. "Tom," I shouted. "What's going on? I've been trying to call you."

Tom stepped out of what would be my room and stood at the top of the stairs. His expression was serious. "Lily, we need you to come up here."

I lifted my foot to start climbing the stairs just as Berto popped his head out of my office. "Lily! Darling. Please, sweetheart, I have a surprise for you."

Berto, my future, or Tom, my contractor? Which to choose first?

I paused, unsure. Tom sounded so serious. Berto was waiting for me. "Tom, I'll be up in a couple of minutes," I called.

His face tightened, but he nodded. "I understand."

Shit, now he was mad, and I still didn't know what the big deal he'd been calling me about was. I tried to smile. "Berto, so good to see you."

He held out his hand, and I took it. With a sexy smile, he pulled me into my office, which had been turned into a romantic dream room. Roses. Candles. Soft curtains. Champagne in an ice bucket with two gorgeous flutes waiting to be filled. "Berto, this is amazing."

"Nothing is too good for you, my love." He kissed me, and it was the longest and most passionate kiss we had ever shared. "I love you and I've missed you."

It had been a good kiss, not a great one. But we could work on that. Maybe he just needed to know what I liked and didn't. I touched his face. "I missed you too."

He dropped to his knees as he held out a small velvet ring box. "Darling, marry me. Let me love you for the rest of your life. Please, marry me."

Shock washed over me, and just behind it came a tidal wave of undeniable nausea. I wrenched myself free in time to see Tom standing in the doorway, his face white with shock or anger as I violently vomited my breakfast all over the antique rug.

Chapter 17

I was horrified. No, that word didn't even begin to cover my mortification. Berto had just proposed, and my response was to vomit all over my own office.

I wasn't sick, and I knew that for sure. And I definitely wasn't pregnant. You generally had to have sex more than once every six months to get pregnant, and I hadn't. Besides, I'd had regular periods since the last time I'd visited David.

What had made me puke like that? Oh, my god, I thew up in front of Tom and Berto, and Berto was still standing there with champagne and a goddamn engagement ring.

I swallowed (hard) because the nausea was still there. With my hand loosely over my mouth, I whispered, "Berto, I am so sorry. Please know I didn't mean to do that, but I do need to clean up, so could you either go home for now, or at least take a walk for a few minutes so I can clean both myself and this room up?"

His eyes glittered. Was that anger I saw in them? His tone was cool. "Of course, Lily. You must have eaten something that upset your system. I will go home, and darling, I will come back up tonight for our dinner, like we planned."

"That would be wonderful." I tried to smile, then realized he couldn't see my mouth as my hand still hovered over it. "Thank you for understanding."

He kissed my forehead. "Darling, we will keep our celebration for tonight."

Berto left without even glancing at Tom, who still stood in the doorway. I looked at Tom, and for the first time since I'd known him, his eyes looked cold and dead. No sparkle, no warmth, no humor. With a shake of his head, he turned away. "I'll get cleaning supplies from the kitchen."

"Tom, no!" I called after him. "I'm the one who got sick; you aren't going to help me clean it up."

"Lily, enough. I'll help you; God knows, I've cleaned up things like this before. When that's done, we need to talk about the project."

"Okay."

He was back in minutes with paper towels, a fresh garbage bag, gloves, and carpet cleaner. Working in silence, we cleaned up the mess. When we were done, I whispered, "Thank you."

Tom was silent. Finally, I looked up at him and saw pure sadness in his eyes. "Lily, I don't understand why someone as amazing as you would let a man like him treat you like that, but clearly you've made your decision."

"What do you mean by that?" I snapped.

"You just got sick, and instead of staying to help you, or at least stay until he was sure you were okay, he confirms he gets his celebration tonight, then he leaves." He shook his head. "You've made your decision, and I'll abide by that. But once we figure out what's going on here, I'm stepping back, other than to supervise the project."

"You can't," I exclaimed.

His voice cut the air like a knife. "I can and I am. You hired my company to get the job done. We will do that. That doesn't mean I have to be here doing it. If that's a problem for you, then I'll give you an updated bill that matches where we are, and you can find another contractor."

"Why are you doing this?"

The anger was back. "Look, if you want a man who will treat you like shit, one who doesn't care about you, one who wants you to conform to his wishes, that's your business. I don't have to stand by and watch it happen."

"Tom, please don't do this. You are the only person other than Berto that I really know around here. Please..." How could I explain I would miss him more than I could say?

He shook his head. "I am your hired hand, Lily. Not your friend. Your contractor. Keep that in mind." He gestured up the stairs. "Now, I really need you to see what is going on here. I've tried for two days to keep it out of the public eye, but eventually, one of my guys is going to get sloppy and spill it to someone. Then it will be a fucking three-ring circus around here."

Chapter 18

We walked up the stairs, with me trailing Tom. He paused at the door of my bedroom. "This is going to be a lot for you to take in, Lily."

I walked into my future bedroom and stopped short. The interior wall nearest the hallway was now open, exposing the framing. Between the studs were at least fifteen paintings in ornate frames. I looked at Tom, my eyes wide. "What is this?"

Tom rolled his eyes. "This is what I've been trying to reach you about for the last two days. When we started to work on the trim around the door, we realized this side was a half inch wider than on the other side. It was done so well that it went undetected—you'd have to know it was there. Once we took the trim off, we could see there was something in the wall."

"They look real," I said as I stepped closer to the first painting. It was a beautiful landscape that looked to be Tuscan.

"I think they are real," said Tom. "I think someone hid them here." He stepped forward and picked up one of the paintings from between the framing. "Look at this one. I think this is an actual Matisse."

"Holy shit," I exclaimed as I looked at the familiar signature in the corner of the canvas. Tom put it back. "We think there could be a lot more of them. We didn't go any further than this room, but looking at the room next door, we think there is a hiding space in that wall too."

"Are you serious?" I nearly shouted the words at Tom.

He nodded. "I am dead serious. Lily, someone hid all of these paintings."

Suddenly, it hit me the seriousness of the situation. "I don't know what we do about this."

Tom paused, then answered firmly. "I think we need to contact the police."

I hadn't considered that as a possibility. "Why?"

"I have to wonder if they weren't stolen."

This was all a bit too much. So far, I had driven back from Montreal, found my boyfriend in my house, he proposed, and I vomited all over my oriental rug. And, yeah, and I seemed to have a secret stash of potentially rare and valuable paintings. I sat down on the window seat and put my head in my hands. "Tom, what do I do? Why are these paintings here?"

"I don't know. I have no idea who would have done this. In my lifetime, no one has ever lived in this house, at least not full time. I don't know who would have done this or why, and I don't know if you were the person who was supposed to find them."

"I guess that's possible," I whispered. "Right now, nothing makes sense."

Tom sat down beside me. "We need to call the state police. We need their input on this."

I nodded. "Do you know anyone we could call?"

"It's best to call the local barracks since this isn't an emergency, but we do need someone to get out here. I'll go make the call."

Even though he was mad at me, he was still helping me, and that was something to be thankful for. "Thanks, Tom. I really appreciate it."

Chapter 19

An hour later, Tom and I were standing again in my future bedroom, now accompanied by two Vermont state troopers. They were as dumbfounded by the find as we were.

Sergeant Nichols finally spoke. "Ms. Brannan, we have no idea what to do with this. I don't think the Vermont State Police have ever had to deal with a case like this before. My recommendation is that we call the FBI's Burlington office for direction."

I nodded in agreement. "I think that's a great idea."

His partner, Lieutenant Jane Beck, looked at me. "Ms. Brannan, do you live here alone?"

"Yes, I do."

Her brow furrowed as she searched for the right words. "Not to say you can't take care of yourself, but I would recommend you have someone stay with you, at least until we get the FBI's recommendations."

"Why?"

"You may have a fortune in paintings here, and knowing that a few other people know about this, I would be concerned for your safety."

I hadn't even thought of that. My shoulders slumped. "I will try to find someone."

A sound very close to a growl came out of Tom's mouth. "Jesus, Lily, I'll stay here until the FBI figures this out. I know the house; I know the property—I'm the best person for it."

"Do you mean it?" I asked.

He rolled his eyes in frustration. "I wouldn't have said it if I didn't."

Lieutenant Beck smiled.

Less than thirty minutes later, the police left, having taken many pictures, and contacted the FBI.

The silence was heavy. Finally, I said, "You don't need to stay, Tom. I'll be fine, okay? And I know how angry you are right now."

Tom didn't look at me. "I said I'd stay, and I will. I've already messaged my mom about keeping Jake tonight, and she'll bring up some clothes for me in just a bit."

Well, that was warm...

"Okay. Well, I really appreciate it."

"I know."

"What do we do now?"

He turned so I could see his face. "I'll keep working, and I expect you'll unpack and take care of everything you need to after being away. I'd also suggest you call your lawyer for any suggestions he may have."

"Good idea."

He looked down at his feet for a second, then gazed at me seriously. "Lily, I know you are getting together with Berto tonight, and I would prefer to not be around for that. If you have him coming here, I'll go out for a bit."

Shit. Berto. In the craziness of seeing those paintings, I'd completely forgotten about him. Jesus Christ, the man proposed to me, and I hadn't thought about him in hours. I swallowed. "Frankly, with everything going on here today, I'm going to call and cancel for tonight."

Tom snorted. "He proposed and you didn't give him an answer. He might take offense if you cancel."

Did I care? It suddenly hit me that I didn't really care if Berto was upset. Okay, that was a problem. Fuck. Here I'd thought I'd come to a decision in Montreal, but now it didn't seem so simple. "I'll deal with that," I said.

"Anyway, I'll be here. After I unpack and call my lawyer, I'll make us some dinner."

"You don't need to, I'll be fine."

Now I wanted to smack him, hard. "For God's sake, Tom, don't be a stubborn ass. I know you're mad at me, and I get it, but we are going to be here together, and we both need to eat."

For the first time since I'd returned from Montreal, Tom smiled. "Point taken."

Chapter 20

It was late afternoon, the sun now setting, and I was trying to edit one chapter before starting dinner. I heard a car coming up the driveway. Looking out the windows by my desk, a state police cruiser comes into view.

Sergeant Nichols and Lieutenant Beck came to the door. "Hi," I said.

It was the sergeant who spoke first. "Hi, Ms. Brannan. We wanted to check on you and give you an update."

"Please come in." We went to my office, where they sat on the couch, I sat at my desk, and Tom took the armchair. "Please, go ahead."

He nodded. "We shared the photos with the FBI and explained the situation. They want to take a look at everything, but they can't get a member of the Art Crime Team here until tomorrow morning."

"And what do they think is going on?"

Lieutenant Beck's gaze was serious. "Ms. Brannan, what do you know about the person you obtained the house from? Can you give us some background to how you came to live here?"

I leaned back in my chair. "My great-aunt Helen left me the house, but I never knew it existed prior to the reading of the will. I knew of everything in that document but this house. Our shared attorney didn't know anything more than I did. And there is no way Helen would have hidden the paintings. If they are genuine, if she had known about them, she would have bragged about them."

Nichols cracked a smile. "You liked her a lot, I gather."

I chuckled. "She was a vicious old bitch. When my mother died, she became my guardian, and she made it clear that she hated me and the responsibility."

Now he laughed. "Okay, well, then... If we assume she didn't put them in the wall, then we need to figure out who she obtained the house from, and why that person or someone else hid them."

"Don't we first need to determine if they are real rather than copies or forgeries?"

"The FBI will handle that. We don't want to announce this to the community. We will wait for the feds to get here."

"Oh." I rubbed my forehead. "What time do we expect them tomorrow?"

"They said they would get to our barracks by nine, then we will come directly here."

"Great." I handed Lieutenant Beck a Post-it note. "That is the name and number of my lawyer, the one who was in charge of Helen's will. He was also the executor of her estate. He will be here by lunchtime tomorrow to help with this process, but if you need to ask him anything between now and then, he will take your calls. That's his personal cell phone number."

They both stood up. "Thank you. We will see you in the morning, and if anything, and we do mean anything, seems out of the ordinary tonight, please call nine-one-one immediately."

"Of course."

Chapter 21

I made dinner while Tom double-checked the locks on the doors and windows. When he came back into the kitchen, he paused in the doorway. "Okay, not my business, but what happened with your plans for tonight?"

I stirred the Alfredo sauce. "I told him something had come up and said I would see him tomorrow."

"And that was it? He didn't press you for an answer?" His voice was a mix of irritation and disbelief.

"No, he said he understood, and we could talk then. I said I'd call him and set a time to meet him in town."

Pulling out forks and knives, he set two places at the counter. "Wow, I'm not sure if I should be shocked or impressed."

"What do you mean?"

He stopped what he was doing to look at me seriously. "I've only proposed once, but I sure as shit couldn't have asked, then waited more than a day to get an answer because of things 'coming up' with a *house*."

I hadn't thought of it that way. I had appreciated how calm and supportive Berto had sounded on the phone. I knew in my heart what my answer was, and I suspected Berto did too, but still, he'd been pleasant as could be. Was that weird? I shrugged. "He didn't know what was happening here, but between me getting sick and telling him something had come up with the project, he was good about it."

"Are you going to accept?"

Fuck. Did I really want to have this conversation with Tom? Didn't I owe it to Berto to talk to him first? I stretched up on my tiptoes to get two pasta dishes and saw my chance to answer while my back was to him. "No," I said.

"Why not?"

That pissed me off. "What do you want from me? You asked a question, I answered you."

"And I only asked why."

"Because..." Why *was* I saying no? I cared about him. He was attractive, and we shared a lot of interests. And the fact was, I did not love him, and I did not think I ever would. "Because I don't love him," I said. "I thought

116

maybe I could over time, but when he proposed, it didn't feel right."

"Was it the violent vomiting that made you realize that?" I could hear the humor in his voice.

Okay, that was funny. I turned around and grinned. "That was the first sign, yes. Then, when you and I were talking about you staying tonight, it hit me that I hadn't thought of him at all while we were wrapped up in the paintings. If I was going to fall in love with him, I would have at least wanted him to be here, right?"

"True."

I plated our dinner. "Come on, let's eat."

Tom opened a bottle of wine while I took the plates to the counter. He handed me a glass. "Cheers."

I raised my own. "Cheers. And thanks for staying."

"No problem."

He took a bite. "This is great, thanks."

"You're welcome."

We ate in silence for a few minutes. Finally, I put my fork down. "Aren't you wondering if I'm going to keep seeing him?"

"No."

"Why not?"

"Look, I asked if you were marrying him. I heard your answer, and while it seems like the relationship is fizzling, I would be a complete ass if I were pressing you about it right now."

"True," I said. "Thanks."

Dinner done, we cleaned up the kitchen. I gestured toward my office. "Want to watch TV for a bit?"

"Sounds good."

"Go on in and pick something. I'll set the coffeemaker for tomorrow then be right in."

"Will do." As Tom walked toward my office, I took a moment to admire his perfect backside. Damn, the man was hot. Was there still a chance for us?

I poured cold water into the coffeemaker then carefully measured the grounds into the basket. I hated having to make coffee in the morning, always had. It was such a little thing, but it made such a difference in my day.

Just then, I heard Tom's voice. He sounded calm, but his choice of words caught my attention. "Lilibelle, ready to come watch television?"

Lilibelle? A wave of fear raced through me. I had never told Tom that was my given name. It wasn't listed anywhere anymore. How could he have known that? I swallowed a mouthful of bile. Something was wrong, really wrong. I cleared my throat and willed myself to sound normal. "Be right there, Tom."

I reached into the cupboard below the sink and felt for the small steel basket I had concealed in the back. There it was, right where it should be.

Yes, I had a gun. Don't judge me; I was a woman who had lived alone in cities for years. I was licensed to own it, and with my small handgun, I was actually a hell of a shot. Here in Vermont? Well, I had brought it along, and after the kitchen was complete, I hid it where only I would know about it. Something was wrong in the next room, and I wasn't going in there unprepared.

Chapter 22

I stuck the handgun into the waistband of my leggings, where it would remain hidden as long as I didn't turn around.

"Do you want anything from the kitchen?" I yelled.

"No, thanks. Just the pleasure of your company."

I walked toward my office, and when I could finally see into the room, my heart jumped into my throat.

Berto was standing in the middle of the room, his back to me. He was facing Tom, who was seated in the armchair again. What the hell was going on?

I remained in the doorframe. "Berto, my love, what are you doing here?"

Berto turned to look over his shoulder at me. Gone was the urbane, refined man I'd come to think I knew. He was disheveled, dressed in black pants and a black hoodie, his hair wild (I could even see there was a twig caught in it.) "Get the fuck in here," he sneered.

What the holy hell? Gone was the soft, Italian-accented English he'd always used. He sounded like someone from South Philly. I tried to pretend I was still relaxed. "What are you talking about, Berto? I told you I would see you tomorrow so we can talk, just the two of us."

He turned a bit more, and suddenly, I could see the large handgun in his hand, pointed directly at Tom.

Okay, badass timing. My almost-fiancé was pointing a gun at my contractor-turned-friend, and the realization hit me—I was head-over-fucking-heels in love with Tom. Not just hot for him, but like (hopefully) happily-ever-after in love with him. Like forever... Like, have-babies-together in love with him.

This was just the perfect time to realize this, right? I had a gun stuck down my pants, Berto (or whoever he was) was pointing a gun at Tom, and I still didn't know what this was all about. Could it be jealousy? "Berto," I whispered cautiously, "is this because I canceled on you tonight? I'm really sorry. Please don't be mad."

He turned fully, the gun now pointed directly at me. "Are you kidding me? I hate you, you spoiled fucking bitch."

My eyes widened. Okay, gun or no gun, he didn't need to be an asshole. "Excuse me? And what's with the American accent?"

"Jesus, Lily, will you stop with the questions? My real name, my given name, is Robert Terrenzini, and I'm from Philadelphia. I did study Italian, and I am a professor, but Berto was a creation of mine. I have a fucking alter ego, okay? I've been in this shithole town for years, for Christ's sake."

"What?"

"Get over here, now. I want to be able to see both of you at the same time."

There were several ways this could be handled, none of them great. I could do as he said, but I had a sneaking suspicion that if I did, we were likely to end up dead. I could pull my gun out and shoot the son of a bitch. (That held some appeal.) I could stand my ground a bit longer and make him look back and forth between us, buying me time to devise a way of keeping my new love interest from ending up like a piece of Swiss cheese.

I was going with that last option. "Okay, Berto, Robert, whoever you are... What is this about? You proposed to me just this morning, and now you're here with a gun. You've made it clear you hate me, so what was your game?"

He was so incensed he seemed to forget he had ordered me into the room. "I've spent my entire life in your fucking shadow, Lilibelle. My entire fucking life. I was the oldest heir, but no, you were the fucking princess."

What the hell was he talking about? Don't tell me I was somehow related to this piece of shit. "I'm lost," I said.

He yelled so loud I could actually feel my eardrums reverberate. "I'm your brother, you bitch! I'm your older brother!"

Wow.

That was unexpected.

Nothing in the prior months had prepared me for that. I had fainted and thrown up when hit with surprises lately. Now, this? What would this do to me?

Wait a second... I was not the least bit nauseous or dizzy.

I was fucking pissed.

Chapter 23

To be fair, it was not exactly what I planned when I chose option three. My plan had been to buy some time while I tried to figure out what to do. But his nasty tone when he said he was my brother? Well, not my finest moment in terms of appropriate responses.

"Brother?" Tom exclaimed.

His voice distracted Berto, who turned his head to snap, "Shut up."

That was all the time I needed. Years of practicing at the range kicked in, and I pulled my gun and nailed the shithead in the calf. (Yes, I was aiming at his calf. I was mad, but not to the point of murder.)

My shot rang out, and he screamed in pain, dropping his gun and collapsing to the floor, clutching his leg. Tom jumped up and grabbed the gun, getting it out of Berto's reach.

Right on cue, red and blue lights lit up the yard. The state police had just arrived.

I should have just stepped back then, putting my hands up, waiting for the police. After all, Berto wasn't going anywhere. He was writhing on the ground, howling in pain, and swearing at me.

Knowing time was up, I took my one opportunity, kicking as I was taught when I played soccer at Miss Porter's, hopefully permanently embedding my brother's balls somewhere up near his sinus cavities.

The unholy noise that escaped Berto told me my kick had found the target. He forgot all about his leg as he rolled into a tight, sobbing ball on the floor. Then, to my delight, he proceeded to vomit all over himself.

He deserved it. You don't tell someone you're their brother and call them a bitch all in the same breath. Asshole.

The police swarmed into the room, grabbing my gun in the process. An EMT wrapped Berto's leg, trying to avoid the copious amounts of vomit he was covered in. Then, the second EMT announced he would need to go to the hospital to get the bullet removed. The police had already cuffed him, and as he lay on the stretcher, Sergeant Nichols took out his notepad. "The EMTs tell me you aren't in mortal danger. You want to tell us your side of the story now, or later at the county jail?"

Berto sneered, which was slightly impressive considering the circumstance. "I want a lawyer."

"I thought you might." Nichols nodded. "Take him away. Make sure he's shackled at the hospital too."

The ambulance drove away as Sergeant Nichols motioned to the couch. "Have a seat," he said.

I'm not good at taking orders, never have been, but considering I had just shot and further assaulted a man, and somehow, I wasn't cuffed, I immediately did what they said. I'm stubborn, not stupid.

Tom sat next to me, and without really thinking about it, I reached out to take his hand. I needed to feel his skin, to know he was still with me. Yes, I now knew how I felt about him, but even beyond that, I was so thankful he had not been hurt because of me. I tried to focus on the police officers. "How did you know to come up here?"

The lieutenant spoke. "Well..."

Nichols rubbed his forehead. "Well, screw it. Just tell her."

Beck tried to hide a smile. "The sergeant's mother called him, having heard on the scanner that we were up here. She told him she'd heard a rumor and it put us into overdrive this afternoon."

I was fascinated. "What rumor?"

Nichols looked straight into my eyes. "That a former Nazi owned this house."

Revulsion filled me, and without meaning to, I dug my nails into Tom's hand. "What are you talking about?"

Nichols removed his hat and held it on his lap. "Lily, my mother said an Italian who supposedly collaborated with the Nazis lived here decades ago. No one had lived here full time since, but that was the rumor."

I swallowed. Shit, that was not what I expected. "And what was the collaborator's name?"

He grimaced. "I think you know the answer to that."

"Terrenzini," I ventured.

"Yup."

I slumped back against the couch, suddenly exhausted and sad. "So, I may have just uncovered my paternal lineage, and if this is right, they were Nazi collaborators. To make it even better, my brother, who knew he was my brother, proposed to me this morning so he could—" I sat up straight. "The paintings," I said.

Beck nodded. "Yes. That's what we think, at least."

"You mean...?"

"We think they are real, and that Terrenzini stole them from Jewish families, smuggled them here, and hid them. We don't know that for certain, but we have asked a search warrant be issued for Berto's house, to see what we can find."

I felt lost. Lost and sad. I had wondered about my father my entire life. If I had any family out there (and it seemed I did), it was a piss poor one. "Okay," I said.

The officers stood up. Sergeant Nichols looked at me with something akin to pity. "I'm sorry, Ms. Brannan. This must be a lot for you. I would still prefer you not be alone tonight in case there are further problems. The FBI will be here first thing tomorrow, and between now and then, maybe we'll learn more about the whole thing."

I stood at the window, watching the cruiser head down the hill. "How did he get into the house?" I asked.

Tom came to stand behind me. "My stupidity," he said. "He called out at the door, and I opened it without looking first because I recognized his voice. If I had seen the way he looked, I would have known something was up. Before I knew it, he was inside, gun in hand. Sorry."

I turned to him in disbelief. "Sorry? Don't be sorry, you gave me the heads up that something was wrong. That was amazing."

He cracked a tiny smile. "Lilibelle?"

"Yeah. How'd you know?"

"He used it when he was sneering about you. I figured since you didn't even have it on your checks or your books, it would tell you something was wrong."

"It did." I closed my eyes as grief hit me. "Only my mom ever called me that. It's on my birth certificate, but that's the only time I see it anymore. If Berto knew it, he's got some real knowledge of me. I knew you were trying to tell me something. Thank you."

"I hoped you would figure it out." He opened his arms silently. Without a thought, I fell into his arms, feeling them wrap me in a wall of safety and comfort.

Then the tears came...

Chapter 24

It was as if all the adrenaline and anger left my body, leaving me with searing sadness and grief.

My mother, my amazing mom, had somehow gotten mixed up with a group of misfits. And, it seemed like I was the descendent of a Nazi collaborator. The man had helped the Nazis hide their crimes, funneled their money to safety, and known what they were doing. Scum. The man was scum.

No, stop that shit. There are no *collaborators*. If you were helping the Nazis, you were a Nazi.

My relatives were Nazis. That's not something I ever thought I would say. And when I finally discovered I may have a brother, he tried to kill me. Great. Family holiday gatherings were going to be a blast.

Did I have a fortune in stolen paintings in my house? What the fuck was that all about?

Finally, the tears slowed. "Thanks," I said.

Tom hugged me. "For what?"

"For not running away screaming from the crazy Nazi lady."

"You're not a crazy Nazi lady." With those words, he snorted, then took my hand. "Come with me."

He led me to the kitchen. "Sit," he ordered, gesturing to one of the stools.

Opening cabinets, he pulled out a bottle of whiskey. "Where do you keep shot glasses?"

"To the left of the fridge."

He got out two shot glasses and filled them, putting one in front of me. "Drink that."

I did. After I finished shuddering, I looked across at him. He took a sip of his, which made me smile. "Thanks."

"You're welcome. It looked like you might need it."

"And you don't?"

That made him laugh. "Okay, well, yes, it's been a hell of a day. But I think I still got the easier side of this."

I rubbed my forehead. "Aren't you going to say I told you so?"

He looked genuinely confused. "About what?"

"About Berto being an asshole."

With that, he slugged back the rest of the shot, grimaced, and put the glass down. "Look, I didn't like him, that's true, but there was no way anyone could have known how bad this seems to be. Give yourself a break, okay?"

He held up the bottle. "Want more?"

"One more, please." He poured and handed it to me, and I took a small sip. "Wow."

"Which part?" He started to chuckle. "The part when the psychopath showed up with a gun? The part where you pulled a gun out and shot him?" He paused. "Damn fine shot, by the way."

"I was aiming for his calf."

He nodded. "I was there, remember? I watched you pull the gun out, sight it, and fire. No shaky hands, nothing. I know where you were aiming, and that's where you hit him."

That made me proud.

"Someday I'll ask you where you learned to shoot like that. But the *pièce de résistance* was when you kicked him." He was clearly trying not to laugh because his voice sounded slightly strangled.

The look on Tom's face made this all seem less important. I grinned, proud of myself. "He deserved it," I said.

"He did, but what the hell was it in that moment that motivated you to kick him?"

"You don't tell someone you are their sister and call her a bitch in the same sentence." I took a swig. "Especially after you proposed to her earlier in the day. Fuckhead."

The mention of the proposal made Tom's face grow serious again. "I'm sorry about that. This must be hard. I know you thought you might have a future with him."

Tom was being so kind and supportive, and I suddenly wanted to smack him for it. "Stop being so noble, for Christ's sake."

That pissed him off. "I'm trying to be supportive," he snapped.

"I know, now knock it off."

He threw his hands up in frustration. "I don't get you," he said. "You wanted me to be okay with being just your fucking lackey while you fucked around with him, so I was trying to do just that, and now you're pissed at me for it. What do you want from me, Lily?"

Should I tell him what I now knew? That I was head over heels for him, probably had been for a while, and that I had almost died from fear when I realized he was in danger because of me? Did I share that now or hold onto it for a while?

Chapter 25

I was just about to tell Tom the truth. The whole truth. Yes, it would be awkward, but it was bubbling up inside me.

Then his phone rang. He picked it up with a sigh. "Hi, Mom."

I could hear her voice through the phone. She was freaking out, that was for sure. Tom was calm. "Yes, Mom, there was an incident up here but we're fine. Berto showed up. Turns out he's not who we thought he was all this time. Yes, the police got involved, and we are sitting here talking about it right now."

I couldn't hear what she said next, but he looked at me and smiled. "Jesus, the gossips are working overtime tonight. Yes, she did shoot him. He'll be fine. He's in custody over at the hospital, and I'm glad you aren't on call tonight because that could have been awkward."

Whatever she replied with made him laugh. "I'll tell her. How's Jake?" There was a pause. "Good, tell him I'll see him tomorrow and I love him." He took a quick look at his watch. "Shit, you're right. No, don't wake him. Love you, too."

He hung up. "Mom says congratulations on shooting him. Based on what she's heard through the grapevine, she's ready to kill him herself."

That made me laugh. "I appreciate the vote of confidence. When they arrest me for it, I may need money for a lawyer, so she may need to start a GoFundMe."

"She'd do it happily."

By now, my urge to tell him everything had waned. The emotion was still there; I just didn't want to start a heavy conversation right now. Maybe tomorrow. I yawned so widely my jaw made a cracking sound.

He stood up and held out his hand. "Come on, princess. Time for you to get some sleep."

I took his hand, loving the way my hand was swallowed up by his much larger one. It gave me an immediate sense of peace.

I was still using my office as a makeshift bedroom. After all, my future bedroom was about to be investigated by the F-B-frigging-I. We walked hand in hand into the office, and I paused. "You can take the couch," I said.

He chuckled. "No, you can sleep in your own bed tonight. And before you offer to let me share it with you because you don't want me sleeping in the chair, the answer is also no."

Did he mean that? Shit.

My face must have shown my internal turmoil. He reached out to stroke a curl off my cheek. "My feelings for you haven't changed over the last few days. But, since you were proposed to in this very room this morning, I think it's best for you to take some time to think about where you're at, and—" his eyes were dark and sexy, and I could feel my insides start to melt "—if I get into that bed with you tonight, I will not be able to remain noble, as you put it."

Well, that was better. He didn't say he didn't like me or didn't want me. He was encouraging me to get my head on straight. That was sweet.

I wiggled a bit. It was sweet and kind. And it wasn't going to help my raging hormones or the ache that was building in me. Berto had seemed attractive to me, but our dynamic had not involved a white-hot, swirling mass of emotion and desire.

Shit, I had it bad. I tried to focus on something other than how much I wanted him in my bed. I nodded. "Thank you."

"You're welcome." He pulled out the couch, flipping it open with ease. He turned down the covers. "Get some sleep."

I pulled my sweater up over my head, leaving just my camisole and leggings on. I slid under the covers and looked up at him.

Tom sat on the edge of the bed and smoothed the covers over me. His touch was gentle, and it made me smile. He leaned over and gazed at me intently. "Could you please get whatever remains of Berto out of your head and heart sooner, rather than later?"

He kissed me, and I knew he felt as strongly as I did. I had never felt this level of emotion and heat with any man.

He pulled back, and I reached up to stroke his cheek. "I will, I promise."

Chapter 26

I woke several hours later; suddenly aware I was not alone in the room. The momentary panic subsided as I realized Tom was stretched out in the armchair, his bare feet resting on the ottoman and an afghan barely covering him. I rolled on my side so I could stare at him in the muted light of the moon that streamed through the cracks in the curtains. Let's face it, I wanted to memorize every inch of him.

I slowly savored the moment. He was so fucking beautiful. And he had figured out a way to protect me today and had stayed tonight, even after all the shit I put him through in the process. He was a keeper, that was for sure.

"You know, I can see you checking me out." He sounded amused.

If he could have seen the color of my skin, my cheeks would have glowed red. "I was not," I countered.

"You were too, and anyway, I did the same to you earlier." He moved in the chair to find a more comfortable spot. "And you need to stop because it is getting harder for me to stay over here."

"You don't need to."

He shook his head. "I do, and you know it."

Sigh. Just when I had finally figured out who I wanted, he developed rules. Sometimes life was not fair. "Fine," I grunted. "Goodnight again."

"Goodnight."

I awoke to the smell of coffee and chocolate. I sat up and realized Tom was no longer in the chair. I struggled out of bed and grabbed clean clothes before heading to the bathroom for a much-needed shower. As I passed the door to the kitchen, I yelled, "Morning, be right back."

"No rush. I'll be here."

I showered quickly but then fussed in front of the mirror. I wanted to look good for him. For weeks, months even, he had seen me in my writing uniform, often after a late night. Usually, I looked, well, like hell. No, not like hell. I'm not bad looking even then, but I certainly didn't look like I genuinely cared about my appearance. Today, I wanted to look like I cared.

A touch of eyeliner, a brush of mascara, and I pulled my hair off my face a bit. I stood back from the mirror. I looked good.

Tom obviously heard me open the bathroom door because when I got to the kitchen, he was pouring me a cup of coffee. I stopped in startled surprise. I was not the only one who had dressed to impress.

Jeans, yes, but not the faded paint-stained ones. A soft blue button-down shirt showed off his physique, and damn, it was a fine one. Rather than his normal work boots, he wore loafers. I suddenly knew exactly what I wanted for breakfast, and it sure as hell wasn't a pastry.

Yup, I was sunk. He looked good enough to eat. Or marry. Or both.

I swallowed. "Hi." Jesus, my voice sounded like it belonged to a wistful fourteen-year-old. I cleared my throat. "Good morning, the coffee smells great."

He grinned, clearly aware of how he was affecting me. "Good. I remembered you said you had brought pastries from Montreal, so they are warming." He gestured to a stool. "Have a seat."

"Thanks." I sat and took a sip of coffee. Should I say it? Shit. "You look really good today."

He stopped in his tracks, halfway to the toaster oven, with two plates in his hand. He put them down, turned, and walked around the counter to me. He turned my stool around and put one arm on either side of me to brace himself before he leaned down.

His breath was warm, and a wolfish smile crossed his face. I could feel myself fight the urge to giggle. "You look good enough to eat. If you're trying to get my attention, Lily, you don't need to work at it, I can promise you that."

I reached up and linked my hands behind his neck to pull him down toward me. Then I kissed him.

I could feel him hesitate for a split second, then he growled and leaned into me, kissing me back. It was perfect. Sexy, hot, and unexpected. I didn't think I could ever tire of kissing this man.

I pulled back, knowing I was about to beg him to take me to bed if I didn't put the brakes on. "Pastries? I swear I heard the word pastry," I said.

He licked his lower lip, and I almost came undone. Shit, the proud look in his eyes showed he knew exactly what he was doing to me. This beautiful, complex man liked to play. Wow, I couldn't wait to finally be his, completely and totally.

We ate breakfast in relative silence, only briefly exchanging social niceties. When we were done, I bounced up off that stool like toast from the toaster. "I'll clean up."

"Okay." He looked at his watch. "I'll call home for a quick check-in, then people should be arriving."

"Sounds good."

Chapter 27

Three hours later, I was alternating between anger, hurt, grief, and bewilderment. My anxiety grew by the second.

I had just come out of the bathroom after brushing my teeth when I heard the first car arrive. Hurrying to the door, I watched James get out of his car, and I almost fell over to see David and Megan were with him. That was going to make things even more awkward with Tom.

Then again, I had to admit that for just a moment, seeing the three of them made me feel safe and loved. They were three people who had been in my corner for a hell of a lot of years. It was good to see them.

Just then, a warm hand settled on my waist. "I'm assuming that's your lawyer," said Tom, "and since I've seen the pictures of your ex, that's him and his wife, correct?"

He sounded calm. Maybe this was going to go better than I thought. "Yes," I said.

Tom chuckled, then dropped his voice to a near whisper, his breath warm on my ear, raising goosebumps on my arms. "Remember what I said."

"What's that?"

He dropped a quick kiss on my bare neck. "I don't share."

I looked up at him through my lashes. "Me either."

He smiled a slow, sexy smile. "Good to know." He stepped back. "I'll give you a moment to say hello without me joining the festivities."

I raced to the car and hugged all three of them joyfully. "James," I exclaimed, "you didn't tell me you were bringing company."

He shrugged. "I thought it was time to bring in the troops. Besides, Megan can help make sure I'm not forgetting something with the FBI. It's always helpful to have co-counsel."

With a spurt of nerves, I motioned to Tom, who walked over, and then I made introductions.

He was charming, shaking hands with each one, commenting on little things I had mentioned about them.

I could see them liking him immediately and him liking them. This might just work!

Then the troopers and FBI arrived. I assumed we would go straight up to the bedroom, but instead, they wanted to talk.

The lead FBI agent was Agent Harrington. Dressed in a dark suit and tie, he looked the part. "Ms. Brannan, we have some information we'd like to share with you."

"Okay."

He opened the black leather portfolio in front of him and handed me a set of papers. "Overnight, the VSP served a search warrant on Mr. Terrenzini's house. They found this letter addressed to you."

I sat back on the couch, looking at the spidery handwriting on the pages in front of me. It was dated almost seven years prior.

My dearest Lilibelle,

There is nothing that grieves me more in my life than to think I had only one opportunity to meet you in person. The day your mother brought you to meet me was the happiest day of my life.

My son Paulo was your father. He had an affair with your mother. At the time, your mother was only seventeen, and Paulo was forty. He also was married with children.

I don't know if he loved your mother, but I do know that to my great dismay, when she told him she was pregnant, he cut her off completely. It was several years after your birth that he finally told me about you, and I was able to contact your mother to offer my support.

Your mother was a woman of rare grace and strength. She wanted nothing from me, having made a life for the two of you. She graciously accepted my letters and sent me information about you, although she would never accept my help in any way. When she died, I would have given anything to raise you myself, but that was not in the cards, as my family was not listed in any way on your birth records.

I had always planned to leave this house to you. When you came here that one time, you ran and played in this house like you had always lived here, and it gave me the greatest joy. We had just removed the stained-glass window from the front hall. You were entranced by that window. I kept it hidden so it would stay safe for what I hoped would be your return to claim your birthright. It is hidden in the walls of what was the master bedroom. I hope you will find it, cherish it, and return it to its rightful place.

That window is not the only secret in this house. For decades, I have kept an ugly and horrible secret, one that I want to share with you, in hopes you will pray for my soul and eventually forgive me.

During World War II, I was still living in Italy. I was a banker and art appraiser then, living well. When the Third Reich started circling our country, I had a decision to make. I *took the coward's choice and helped those in that evil empire. I help let them know of the art collections held by clients, and they then seized those works from any members of the Resistance or Jews.*

I could see what was happening. I did nothing to stop it. I am so ashamed of that. But then, in an effort to protect myself and my own, I did something I can never forgive myself for. I stole works of art myself, keeping them hidden until I could get them out of the country to bring here.

When I bought this house, it was for two reasons. One was for the beauty and solitude it provided. The other was that I knew I could hide the pieces here and keep them safe for the future.

In this house, I have hidden the stained-glass window and twenty-three paintings. Each of the paintings is listed on the following pages, along with the provenance, and where I acquired it. I have listed the names of the rightful owners of those treasures.

This house is yours. It was the only legacy I had to give you. The paintings are yours to do with what you will. I know you will do what is right.

Every letter your mother sent included a picture of you. Those pictures were the greatest gifts I received. I loved you from the second I knew of your existence, and I wish we could have known each other well in person.

147

I will always be with you, my beloved granddaughter. I am so proud of you, and I love you more than I can tell you.
With all my love,
Angelo Terrenzini, your nonno

My eyes were huge as I looked up after leafing through the enclosed papers. "He stole the paintings."

Agent Harrington nodded. "Yes, and we also found more information in Robert's house. He had known something was up, having known what his grandfather had done and where he'd lived, and he tried for years to find the paintings. Then, when his father—" he paused "—your father, died, he found this letter. That was a couple years ago, so he went into overdrive. When you arrived, he wanted to find the paintings before you did."

"Jesus."

"So, we know you have twenty-three paintings here. We know you've found fifteen of them, so we need to uncover the rest."

James interrupted. "And what happens then?"

The other agent, Agent Thomas, answered. "Then we take custody of them, have an expert authenticate them, and determine what happens then."

It took hours, but we finally found the last set of paintings hidden in a wall off the dining room. Everyone gathered in the dining room for the FBI to take photos. I stood there and gazed at them. They were gorgeous, and yet the ugly history associated with them made me queasy. I didn't know how to feel. I had a grandfather, and he had loved me. He had done horrible things, and yet he hoped I would make it right. I had a father who didn't want anything to do with me. I had a brother who had tried to trick me into letting him into the house. Jesus, no wonder I was exhausted and confused.

Tom's hands were gentle on my shoulders. "Come with me."

"Why? I should stay here."

"Come on."

I followed him silently as he walked outside to the big rock behind the barn and sat down. I sat too. He took my hand. "You okay?"

That was it. Those two words were my undoing, and I started to sob.

Without a word, Tom pulled me into to his arms and let me cry.

Chapter 28

Hours later, I sat at the kitchen counter, surrounded by a pizza box and empty wine bottles. James, David, Megan, and I had just eaten a lot of pizza and washed it down with more than a reasonable amount of wine.

Tom had gone home, not wanting to be away from Jake for two dinners. I missed him already.

After I had cried, he wiped my tears and told me it would all work out. Then he put a finger under my chin. "And," he said, "when this is all over, will you please go out with me?"

That was the best thing I had heard all day.

I cleared the debris from dinner. James handed me the empty bottles, which I dropped into the recycling bin. He looked concerned. "So, you understand what is happening, right?"

I nodded. "Yes, the FBI took control of the paintings. If they can prove they are legitimate, and then find the original families, they will be returned."

"Right."

"And you'll be the contact person."

"Yes. And the security team is coming tomorrow to set up the alarm system. If the press wants to talk to you, refer them to me. Got it?" said James.

"I got it."

I walked into the office and grinned when I saw David at my computer, scrolling through my recent work. "Looks good, Lil. Too much dialogue in that last chapter though."

It felt good to hear that. Life might someday return to normal after all. "Fuck you," I teased.

Megan sat in the armchair with a work file in front of her. She looked up and peered at me over her readers. "So, what's the deal with Tom?"

I smiled. "He's amazing."

"Then get off your ass, bestie, and make him yours."

Chapter 29

Once Megan and David left for the evening to go to a local motel for the night, I locked up. James insisted on keeping an eye on me, so we made up a bed on the office floor. "I don't see why we can't sleep in the same bed as we always do," he half-teased.

I grinned. "Because I want to make this work with Tom, and he wouldn't understand such a thing."

He chuckled. "Then at least make sure there's a guest room the next time I visit."

"Of course."

I lay in bed thinking about Megan's words. Was it time to truly make a move on Tom? What did I want from him? For him?

I sat up, knowing exactly what I wanted. It was time to make it happen. "James," I hissed.

He roused from what was clearly a sound asleep. "What?"

"I'm going to run into town to see Tom. I'll be back soon."

He sat up. "Okay. Drive carefully." He paused. "Does this mean I can have your bed?"

If all went well, I wouldn't be back home tonight. "You sure can."

I drove through the dark roads with what felt like butterflies multiplying in my stomach. What would I do if he turned me down?

I stopped a block away and called him. He answered on the second ring. "Are you okay?" he said.

"I am." I tried to find the right words. "I'm nearby, can I come over?"

"Of course."

I pulled into his driveway and turned the car off. It was now or never.

Tom was sitting on a porch swing. He looked at me curiously. "Hey," he said.

"Hey."

He patted the bench beside him. "Want to join me?"

"Please." I sat. "Thanks."

He waited in silence. I took a deep breath. "I need to tell you something."

"Okay."

The words came out in a rush. "I thought a lot about you when I was in Montreal, but then I perceived Berto to be the easiest, most logical path. I never deluded myself into thinking I was in love with him, but I thought it was worth trying. But when he proposed, all I could think about was the look on your face. In that moment, you were the one I cared about."

"Oh."

"And then when I saw you were in danger last night, it hit me like a ton of bricks. I was so afraid he might hurt you, I wanted to kill him."

His tone was cautious. "What are you saying?"

I knew exactly what I wanted to say. "I'm saying that I'm in love with you. I want you to be in my life for the rest of it. I want to be Jake's mom; I want to have babies with you. I want to make a family and a life with you." I took his hand, hoping he wasn't about to break my heart. "Would you please marry me?"

Tom leaned back, then reached out to stroke my cheek. "Are you proposing to me?"

"What's the matter, haven't you ever been proposed to?"

"Never."

"So, what do you think?" I said.

Tom stood up, and before I knew what was happening, he had dropped to his knee. "Lily Brannan, there is nothing I want more in this world than to spend the rest of my life loving you. Yes, I will marry you."

I leaned forward. "I love you."

"I love you, too." With that, he pulled me into his arms and kissed me.

I was wrong; that first kiss with him wasn't the greatest kiss in human history, this one was. This was exactly where I was supposed to be, and he was the man for me. Finally, I pulled back. "And just to be clear, I don't frigging share."

That made him laugh. "You won't ever have to, Lily, that I promise you."

Wrapped in his arms, I reached up to link mine around his neck. "So, now can I spend the night?"

"On the couch?" The twinkle was back in his eyes. "Too tired to drive home?"

"Not tired at all, just..." The truth took my breath away, and tears suddenly welled up in my eyes. "I don't ever want to sleep without you again, ever."

Gently, he brushed away the lone tear on my cheek. "You won't have to, love." With that, he stood up, and holding me tightly in his arms, strode inside. "Let's go start our lives together."

Epilogue

I chuckled as I entered our hotel suite in New York. Jake was almost six now and thought he ruled the world. He was currently jumping on the bed like a wild man. Baby Violet, just a year old, was lying on a blanket in the sunshine while her daddy tickled her stomach.

"Mommy," Jake screamed, and he stopped jumping to hold out his arms to me.

I kissed his forehead as I hugged him. "Hi, buddy."

Tom reached out to take my hand. "How did it go?"

"Great. The exhibit is ready for the opening."

While all the paintings had been reunited with heirs from their rightful owners, working with the families, I had arranged for the entire group to be exhibited for one month to raise Holocaust awareness. The exhibit was set to open tomorrow night here in New York, and we had traveled down from Vermont to be there for the opening.

Tom got to his feet and kissed me slowly. "I'm so proud of you," he said. "You took an awful situation and made something good come out of it."

"I couldn't have done it without you." I nibbled on his lower lip. "Later, I'll show you how grateful I am."

His deep chuckle heated my blood like it always did. My husband still rocked my world, still was my world, and I knew that would never change. His voice was low, "Can't wait."

Acknowledgments

Thanks to Sutton and Cyn for their amazing work as editors. Thanks to Between the Lines Publishing for being such the best publishing house, and to Cherie for her amazing artwork.

Kris Francoeur, writer and educator, lives in Vermont with her family and a menagerie of interesting creatures. Kris also is a grieving mother, who has found joy and light again through the practices of conscious and deliberate gratitude, unconditional acceptance, and connection with nature. Kris writes with authority about grief and moving forward in our very busy and stressful world, as well as being an accomplished author of contemporary novels, and a successful ghostwriter. Kris loves to spend time with her family (including sons, daughter, and grandchildren), spending time in the garden and spinning the alpaca fiber for yarn for knitting.

CPSIA information can be obtained
at www.ICGtesting.com
Printed in the USA
LVHW092325030922
727569LV00014B/1242

9 781958 901014